PRAISE FOR VINCENT

"Sensational...masterful...br

"My fear level rose with this ...e it hasn't done before. Wondering what the k...er had in store for Jude and seeing the ending, well, this is one book that will be with me for a long time to come!"
—Reviews by Molly

"I very highly recommend this book...It's a great crime drama that is full of action and intense suspense, along with some great twists...Vincent Zandri has become a huge name and just keeps pouring out one best seller after another."
—Life in Review

"(The Innocent) is a thriller that has depth and substance, wickedness and compassion."
—The Times-Union (Albany)

"I also sat on the edge of my seat reading about Jude trying to stay alive when he was thrown into one of those games...Add to that having to disarm a bomb for good measure!"
—Telly Says

"...a gripping psychological thriller that will keep you riveted on the edge of your seat as you turn the pages."
—Jersey Girl Book Reviews

"This book is truly haunting and will stay with you long after you have closed the covers."
—Beth C., Amazon 5-star review

"The action never wanes."
—Fort Lauderdale Sun-Sentinal

"Gritty, fast-paced, lyrical and haunting."
—Harlan Coben, bestselling author of *Six Years*

"Tough, stylish, heartbreaking."
—Don Winslow, bestselling author of *Savages*

CHASE BAKER
AND THE
GOD BOY

(A Chase Baker Thriller #3)

VINCENT ZANDRI

Bear Media LLC 2015
4 Orchard Grove, Albany, NY 12204
http://www.vincentzandri.com

Cover design by Elder Lemon Art
Author Photo by Jessica Painter

ISBN-13:
ISBN-10:

Published in the United States of America

"There is no death. How can there be death if everything is part of the Godhead? The soul never dies and the body is never really alive."

—Isaac Bashevis Singer

"Thuggees were an organized gang of professional assassins – sometimes described as the world's first terrorists – who operated from the 13th to the 19th centuries in India. Members of the fanatical religious group were infamous for their ritualistic assassinations carried out in the name of the Hindu Goddess Kali. According to the Guinness Book of Records, the Thuggees were responsible for approximately two million deaths."

—Ancient Origins

1

The Fiddler's Elbow
Piazza Santa Maria Novella
Florence, Italy
October 2015

"**THE PROBLEM WITH YOU AMERICANS, MATE, IS YOU** think you're entitled to the world."

The man who presently has his hand wrapped around my neck is Scottish or, what some people refer to as, a Scott. He's also much bigger than me, drunk as a rabid skunk, and really pissed off, which doesn't bode well for my immediate future.

"I work for a living," I say, my words coming out more like *I-wor-fer-a-livin'*, what with my wind-pipe about to be crushed. "Nobody's givin' me a thing." Or, *Nobies-giv-a-thin...*

The issue here is not one of governmental policy-making, nor are we engaged in a geopolitical, socio-economical debate regarding the United States of America and its lone world power status. Instead, we're playing an innocent game of Blackjack, which up until now we've been engaging in rather pleasantly at the old wood bar. That is, before I made the mistake of spotting Calum slip an extra Ace under his dealt cards when he assumed I wasn't looking.

Problem one is that Calum is drunk—really soused and not exactly adept at sleight of hand. Problem two is that the normally mild-mannered freelance English/Italian teacher is also a retired mercenary who once fought for the French Foreign Legion in the Balkan Wars, the Persian Gulf Wars, and more recently, Iraq and Afghanistan. Oh, and problem three, did I fail to mention that in retaliation for his cheating I picked Calum's stash of cash up off the bar and stuffed it into the pocket of my khaki work shirt?

Six feet tall, round face covered with a thick red beard, bearing the shoulders of a rugby fullback, Calum (last name unknown), might never see forty again, but he's fully capable of tossing me through the barroom window. Which is precisely what he's proceeding to do right this very second.

He releases his hold on my neck, uses one hand to pick me up by the collar of my leather jacket, and the other to grab hold of my belt like I'm a bail of Highlands hay he's about to toss into the back end of a horse drawn cart.

"Cal, buddy," I say. "This isn't right. You were cheating. What's fair is fair, don't you agree?"

"Toss him, Cal," comes a voice from the crowd inside the bar. "Toss his American ass back to Obama."

My friends...What senses of humor...

But then I hear, "Calum, put Chase down this very instant!"

It's Matt, the Fiddler's Elbow owner and proprietor. I catch a quick glance of the tall, wiry, middle-aged man. He's wearing a black T-shirt that bears the white letters ABCD in AC/DC-style logo.

"I'm tossing the bastard," Calum says in his heavy brogue. "Ayyy, he called me a cheater. He stole me money."

"A round for Calum Whatever-your-last-name-is," I shout as he raises me up so that I'm not only facing the window, I'm seeing the reflection of my closely cropped hair, stubble-covered face, and terrified, wide brown eyes.

"Too late, Baker," he says. "You insult me, you insult me entire clan."

He swings me backward to create a pendulum effect, so that when he finally decides to let me go I will literally fly through the window.

"One!" the bar crowd shouts.

I'm propelled forward. But the man-bear isn't quite ready to release me.

He swings me backward again.

"Two!!!" they shout, enjoying my imminent demise far more than they are the soccer match being broadcast on four separate wall-mounted flat screens...Oh, wait, not soccer. Futball.

I swing forward again so that the top of my head nearly touches the glass. And back again.

"Threeee!" the crowd shouts.

"Calum!!!!" Matt screams.

I close my eyes, feel myself propelled forward like a cannonball shot out of a cannon.

Oh shit...

Here's the surprising thing: Getting tossed through a window, as dramatic and cinematic as it might appear in the movies, isn't all that bad. What *is* bad, is landing on the cobblestone sidewalk on the other side of it. Luckily, I'm wearing my worn leather jacket over my work shirt or the skin on my chest, arms, and palms would mimic raw hamburger for certain. But the impact of human being against cobblestone does knock the air out of me so that when the still very pissed off, and apparently never satisfied, Calum, exits the Elbow through its open front door, bulling his way through the onlookers, I can't even hope to put up a fight. All I can possibly manage is to roll over like a dog, raise my arms up in surrender from down on my back. What the hell, maybe he'll give me a belly rub.

But even a white-flag maneuver like surrender doesn't stop the former French Foreign Legionnaire from lowering himself onto one knee, making a fist with a hand the size of the Loch Ness monster, cocking it back. Squeezing my eyelids closed, I await the death blow.

But it never comes. In its place comes a gentle, if not haunting voice.

"You will not harm that man any longer."

The voice isn't deep, but it isn't high either. The tone is soft and peaceful, like the sound of a gentle breeze blowing off a calm lake. The accent isn't Italian or anything European for that matter. More like American. Maybe even New Yorkian. The East Coast anyway.

I open my eyes to see a silhouette of a man. A big man, who stands over me, the high afternoon sun positioned directly behind his back. The dark figure is imposing, the head shaped more like a bullet or a howitzer shell, the apex coming to a distinct, sharp peak. It isn't until he bends down, offers me his hand, that I see his face and realize he's wearing a black and gold turban.

"Mr. Chase Baker, I presume," he says politely, gallantly.

"Uh huh."

He kneels down, offering me his hand.

"My name is Iqbal...Dr. Iqbal Lamba Singh. They told me I would find you here."

"Who's they?"

"The Florence Police and Fire Brigade."

"They know me so well I guess."

He smiles warmly, his smooth tan face gentle but intense at the same time. I take his hand and he pulls me up like he's capable of dead-lifting a sacred cow.

"Back off, Haji," Calum shouts. "This one's mine, ayyy.'

Dr. Singh does something extraordinary. He turns completely around and faces down Calum. At first, the former Legionnaire clenches his fists, raising the right one, cocking it back at the elbow like he's about to lay my turban-wearing savior out. But Dr. Singh stands his ground, arms relaxed at his sides, fingers open, legs slightly spread at shoulder length. Eyes wide, he initiates a staring contest with Calum. It's as if the doctor's gaze is a tractor beam that locks not onto Calum's blue eyes, but into them. Into his Guinness-soaked his brain. The soldier turned piss poor card shark can't avert his gaze even if he wants to.

The entire crowd of onlookers falls silent as if Piazza Santa Maria Novella were placed on pause by God himself. After a long, drawn-out moment, Dr. Singh raises his right hand, holds out his palm, five stick-like fingers extended vertically.

"You will not harm Mr. Baker," he says in a commanding tone. "You will turn and leave this place at one."

"Wait," Matt chimes in, pushing his way through the crowd. "What about my window?"

"Calum," Dr. Singh says.

Calum stands flat-footed, caught up in a robotic, almost zombie-like trance.

"You will pay for a new window. And you will never raise your fist against Mr. Baker again. Do you understand?"

It only takes two or three Guinness pints to turn Calum's face red beneath his beard. But Dr. Singh's words make him go visibly pale. For a second, I'm convinced he might toss the dozen pints he'd just consumed over the course of three hours all over the tourist crowded piazza. His burly arms and chest seem suddenly deflated, like a bloated haggis that's been poked. He shakes his head, turns, and begins to walk slowly away.

"Ayyyyy...I understand," he mumbles in a semi-sedated, trance-like state, eyes wide open. "Me apologies, Chase. Beer's on me next time."

Dr. Singh turns back to me, purses his lips.

"That man will never harm you from this moment on," he insists. "In fact, he will always be in your debt."

The crowd issues ooohs and ahhhs, as if they just witnessed the most fascinating circus sideshow on earth. A group of surgically masked Chinese tourists clap.

"How'd you do that?" I ask the mysterious, tall, dark man named Singh.

"Perhaps we can go somewhere and converse alone," he suggests.

"You got a job in mind?"

"Almost certainly."

"You like beer?"

"I prefer tea."

"No surprise there," I say. "Follow me."

Together we head out of the piazza, my breast pocket still stuffed with Calum's cash.

WE MAKE OUR WAY THROUGH THE CENTRAL market, past the cheap tourist eateries, past the gypsies begging for coin in the name of Christ, past the Iranian leather merchants, and over a narrow side street that houses grocery stores owned and operated by West Africans who spend their afternoons drinking away their beer inventory. Coming to a street called Via Guelfa that runs perpendicular to the side street, I instruct Dr. Singh to go right, which he does. Ahead is a small café that's mostly patronized by students and faculty of the nearby America University. It's a smart place to sit and talk. Dr. Singh seems like one smart dude.

We take an empty table outside. He orders tea and I order an espresso. I sit and ponder where this character came from until the drinks arrive, soaking up a late afternoon that is neither too hot nor too cool, the creative bustle that's always made Florence so attractive to creative types for a thousand years going on all around us.

"You must be pondering many, many questions, Mr. Baker," Dr. Singh says after a time, taking a small, careful sip of his hot tea. "Not the least of which is who am I and why have I sought you out?"

"Be a good place to start," I say, drinking down my espresso in one swift pull. Chase Baker, man of international adventure and espresso junkie. "But first, I want to know how you pulled off that little stunt back there. After fighting more wars than I have fingers on my right hand, Calum's sort of off his rocker if you know what I mean. I'm pretty sure he was about to clean the piazza cobbles by using me as a dish rag."

He sips more tea.

"My family name is Singh," he says. "Which in India means I am a Sikh. Sikhs are warriors by tradition."

"But you're American. Talk like one anyway."

"Indeed. Born in Varanasi but raised in Manhattan. My father taught biophysics at New York University. However, my family ties are strong, and it's because of those ties that I have learned the practice of what you might recognize as the evil eye."

"That's how you tamed the savage beast? The evil eye? Isn't that just a myth?"

He laughs gently. "It's not really evil, and it's not as mysterious or mythical as all that. You see, my background is psychoanalysis and psychotherapy. It's actually a hypnotic maneuver that doesn't take all that much skill once you learn the technique."

He presses his lips into a grin, but my built in

truth detector tells me immediately this man isn't happy. Not by a long shot.

"Dr. Singh," I say after a beat, "what is it you want from me?"

He reaches into the pocket on his long, button-down shirt, pulls out a photograph. He sets the photo down on the table for me to see. Initially, the full-color image doesn't register in my still slightly buzzed brain. But very quickly it takes shape. When I realize what I'm looking at, I feel my pulse pick up speed.

"Mr. Baker," he says, "I would like to introduce you to my beautiful five-year-old son, Rajesh."

To say the boy is abnormally constructed is an understatement of gargantuan proportions. This boy doesn't possess a single set of arms. Instead, he was born with one set of arms that protrude from his shoulders like any normal person, but also two more sets that emerge from his mid and lower torso, respectively. He looks almost like a human spider, or maybe a scorpion.

What's even more remarkable about the boy is that he is dressed in the princely clothing of the traditional Indian aristocracy—a Nehru jacket covered in gold stitching, matching pajama-like pants, and a Sikh turban inlaid with the identical gold stitching. He's also sporting matching earrings made of brilliant green jade. In the photo, he's smiling like not a thing is wrong or out of synch with both his spiritual and physical world.

Me, I'm exhaling, wishing I had a stiff drink to wash all this down with. "What caused this, Dr. Singh? How can something like this happen?"

"Rajesh was born five years ago with a birth defect which can occur when two or more embryos gestating in the mother's womb die, leaving only one survivor.

In such circumstances, the living sibling inherits the underdeveloped remains of the once co-joined embryos. This parasitic embryo manifests itself in the form of additional limbs that are attached to the torso. The condition is a one in a million occurrence, or so my extensive research reveals. But then, thirty-four babies are born every minute in India. The law of odds dictates that not every one of them will be perfect. Or, looking at the situation another way, perhaps Rajesh is the ultimate manifestation of perfection."

My eyes on the photo. Glued to it.

...*I prefer the imperfection of just two arms*...

"Is the condition painful?"

Shakes his head slowly, deliberately. He's been asked this question a thousand and one times prior. "No pain. However...I say this with great sadness...children like Rajesh do not live long. Multiple limbs place undue strain on the heart and circulatory system. Structurally speaking, there are spinal problems, muscle weakness, excessive fatigue."

"I'm sorry, Dr. Singh. You must be broken-hearted. But what gives? Why are you showing me this?"

"You see, Mr. Baker, in my country a child born with one or more limbs can initially be considered an outcast, which at one time, Rajesh was. His mother and I were forced to shield him from the outside world or else face unimaginable ridicule."

"People are assholes."

His eyes light up.

"Excuse my French, Doc."

He appears to be suddenly aghast. A man who's clearly not used to being one of the guys.

"But then something else happened to Rajesh," he goes on. "News of his condition leaked to a nearby collection of Jain Dharma, who did not consider him a freak of nature, but instead, something extraordinary. They consider him a living god."

"Jain Dharma?"

"Purists who walk the earth without clothing, and depend entirely upon handouts for their very existence. They assume the five major vows." Raising the fingers on his hand, dropping one finger per vow. "Non-violence, non-stealing, honesty, chastity, and non-attachment."

"They're always naked? Sounds like some of my girlfriends at the Elbow."

"Yes. Always naked. The representative symbol of Jainism is something that might shock you as a westerner, Mr. Baker."

"Try me."

Extending his index finger, he runs it through the condensation that's collected on the tabletop, sketching out the symbol. The sketch he produces makes me slightly nauseous considering the extended family I lost in World War II, not to mention six million Jews exterminated over their religious beliefs.

"The swastika," I say.

"The ultimate symbol of peace. Stolen by the Nazis...bastardized. Nearly ruined."

"The naked swastika guys see Rajesh as a God." It's a question.

"The reincarnation of the Hindu God, Brahma, in fact. What this means is, Rajesh has gone from causing shame to his family and village to being revered by all who lay their eyes upon him. For this reason, I've had to deal with a very new and very different concern over keeping him away from public gatherings. Until recently that is, when his existence could be shielded no longer."

I steal another glance at the picture. "He doesn't seem entirely unhappy."

"Indeed, he is famous now. And wealthy, for Indian standards. Even your *New York Times* and *USA Today* has picked up on Rajesh's story. Wherever he goes, he attracts huge crowds of worshippers. Many people come from miles around to receive just a quick glimpse of him. The hungry come to be fed. The sad come to be happy again. The sick and the infirmed come to be healed. He lays one or more of his hands on them, and they experience something out of this world."

"But, of course, it's just an illusion," I say. "Mind over matter. He's not really a God. He just plays one on TV, right?"

He nods. "Under normal circumstances, I might agree with you. After all, I was educated in the states...at Harvard, and I am in possession of multiple psychology-related degrees, as I mentioned. We have little room for hocus pocus, religion, or mysticism in my working world. It is a field pertaining to the nuances and chemical reactions inside the greatest mystery known to mankind...the human brain." He pauses to take a breath. "But something is different with Rajesh. His condition is not just physical, Mr. Baker. It is, let's say, out of this world."

"You saved my life, Doc, and now you've my attention."

He lifts up his tea again. This time when he does, his hand is trembling as if in his revealing the sacred truth about Rajesh, he has bared his very soul. He sets the cup down without drinking.

He says, "Rajesh *has indeed* healed people, Mr. Baker. I've seen it with my own eyes. He has healed the infirmed, made the blind see again. He has even…" His voice trails off as if what he's about to say is too painful for words. Or too unbelievable maybe.

"Go on," I say.

He stares into his tea for a while. Until he raises his head, peers into my eyes with his big brown eyes.

"With his touch, he has given new life to the dead," he says.

My mind races with the possibilities. I've been to India. With my dad when we were sandhogs for some of the archeologists working along the northern border with Nepal. I know first-hand that India is a land of reincarnation. Where death is celebrated as much as life. I've witnessed men and women who are transported to what will be the site of their burial by fire along the banks of the Ganges days, sometimes weeks, before their hearts cease to beat. This is not a callous or even morbid act. It is instead a celebration. People do not die in that vast, congested land, so much as they are reborn. Flesh and blood dies and burns. Souls live on.

But I've never before heard of a child, regardless of how many limbs he was born with or how much he mimics the legendary appearance of Brahma or Kali, raising someone from the dead. That act was reserved for one historical man and one man only.

Jesus of Nazareth.

It's precisely how I put it to Dr. Iqbal Lamba Singh.

"You are correct about that," he says. "But did you know that evidence exists of Jesus's travels in Nepal and India? Between his twenty-fifth and thirtieth year, there is a strong possibility that he studied with the Jainists, became indoctrinated in their belief system, and at the same time, became a master of Indian mysticism. Something he applied with great success and also great tragedy to his ministry once back in Jerusalem."

"If that's true, then Jesus did not raise Lazarus, or even himself, because of his connection to a Hebrew God. He acted on behalf of Brahma."

"Just like Rajesh. Like the historical Jesus, I have seen him heal the blind by applying an eyepatch of mud created of loose earth mixed with his own saliva. I've seen him cure a malignant tumor just by laying his hands upon it. I have seen him create many loaves of bread from one single loaf. You just don't forget such instances, Mr. Baker."

"Have you seen the kid turn water into booze?" I smile. "Now, there's something I'd like to see."

The man just stares at me, like my comment is entirely inappropriate. And I suppose it is. In any case, I find myself biting down on my bottom lip. Something I always do when nervous, or my interest is entirely piqued, which it most definitely is.

"So what's the end all to this, Dr. Singh? Why did you rescue me from my lovely afternoon of drinking beer and playing cards if you wanna call it that? Why are you telling me all this?"

"Mr. Baker, I have read your books and also read about your exploits in Egypt and the Amazon Jungle. I know what you are capable of both as an investigator and as a man who fears nothing."

Raising my hands, making a time-out T.

"I am most definitely not fearless, Dr. Singh," I say. "Christ, I don't even like to fly...Damn, sorry about the Christ reference."

He issues the subtlest of smiles. A man not without a sense of humor, but also a man who takes pride in his dignity.

"It is okay. I do not consider my boy the modern

Christ. Instead, I consider him the gifted flesh of his very mortal parent's flesh, and they love and miss him so very much."

My truth detector lights up. "What do you mean they miss him?"

"In answer to your question of why you are here with me now," he says, "Rajesh is missing. Gone. Kidnaped by those who wish to abuse his power for their own dark purposes."

"Who precisely?"

"The Thuggee and their black-hearted God, Kali."

I GET UP FROM THE TABLE, PUSH IN MY CHAIR.

"Look, Dr. Singh, I know precisely where this is going. Like I told you, I'm good with finding missing people, and I've even been known to dig up an archeological relic now and again. But I do not, will not, battle a satanic cult that will string me up and dissect me alive as easily and thoughtlessly as cooking up some chicken tandoori on the grill. Only thing that distinguishes the Thuggee from ISIS is they've been around far longer and have perfected their killing techniques. If my history serves me right, they were responsible for the slaughter of more than two million innocent souls before the British put an end to them in the mid-nineteenth century." I start walking on Via Guelfa towards my home. "Thanks for saving my ass at the bar and thanks for the coffee, but

I'm not your man. You need the fucking *Expendables*...excuse my French times two."

"Mr. Baker!" he shouts, so loud his voice echoes off the old stone and stucco-faced five-story buildings.

I turn to find him standing by the table. "There is something I'm not telling you that might change your mind."

"What exactly is that?"

He stares not at me, but into me. His eyes not blinking, drawing me into their powerful gaze like he managed to do with psycho-Calum only minutes before.

"Elizabeth," he says. "Elizabeth Flynn."

The name hits me like a sledgehammer to the head. A name that goes with a face I've tried my damnedest to forget about over the last five years.

"How do you know that name?" Gravel in my voice, profound heaviness in my heart.

"Let's go someplace and talk more. This is not the place."

A car passes. Then a motorbike. Following that a truck. Foreign exchange and Junior Year Abroad Students fill the sidewalks with their school bags slung over their shoulders. The bells inside Giotto's Tower in nearby Piazza del' Duomo are tolling the five o'clock hour. They toll for me. Ominous rings to say the least.

"Elizabeth," I say, the name slipping off my tongue like warm water. It's a name I have not uttered out loud since the day I left her on a train platform in the Varanasi station, but a name I have no doubt spoken countless times in my mind and in my sleep. It's also a name I heard again, just last month, in a disturbing letter that I received at my Florence address. But now, this...

"I can lead you to her probable whereabouts."

"But that's impossible, Singh. She's dead."

"No one dies, Mr. Baker. Not really. Perhaps we should talk more."

The cobbles beneath my feet feel like they're turning to liquid. This conversation is creepier and creepier with each vowel uttered.

Don't do it, Chase. Don't take the bait...Don't... You...Do...It!

"Follow me," I say, my mouth suddenly gone dry. So much for resolve. Chase the weak and the whipped.

As Dr. Singh approaches me, I turn away so that he doesn't see the tears welling up in my eyes.

4

IT'S A THREE-MINUTE WALK TO MY SECOND-FLOOR apartment on Via Guelfa. But in that time, I relive an all-too-short lifetime of memories with Elizabeth. Our meeting in Paris. Me just coming off a particularly difficult dig in Turkey, having assisted in uncovering an underground city in the Nevsehir Province and trying to make an overdue novel deadline. Her trying to work up cash for her one and only project: The precise location of the legendary Golden Kali Statue.

The statue was said to be important not only as a priceless piece of man-sized gold statuary but also for the map it supposedly contained on its upper back. Legend has it that the map illustrates the exact whereabouts of the infamous India blue diamond deposit. Folklore to be sure. Hell, maybe even fantasy. But a fascinating prospect all the same.

There was more to the puzzle. A kind of key that accessed the interior of the statue. And Elizabeth was in possession of it. But what secrets the interior of the Kali Statue held, nobody knew. Without the statue, the key was nothing more than a useless piece of ancient jewelry. It wasn't a key in the traditional sense, but instead a four-inch long by one-inch wide piece of bronze with dozens of diamond chips embedded inside it. Elizabeth had discovered it, of all places, in a family-run antique shop in Rome, Italy. She purchased it for two-hundred Euros, the owner having no idea of its real worth. But if it were the authentic key to the true Kali statue, then its value was potentially priceless.

But I'm getting ahead of myself. Way ahead.

As I approach my apartment, I spot several young couples seated at a little round table at an outdoor bar, drinking wine, smoking cigarettes, engaged in passionate conversation with smiles on their faces. Smiles that tell me their future is unwritten and, from the vantage point of their tables, entirely rosy. As it once seemed for Elizabeth and I, when we first met.

She already occupies a stool inside the sparsely populated Paris Ritz Bar Hemingway when I come in for a late afternoon '76er, one of my favorite summertime cocktails. She's chatting it up with Colin— the bar's tall, semi-bald, white jacket-attired proprietor—while I ask her if the seat beside her is taken.

"By all means," she says in an American accent, brushing back shoulder-length strawberry blonde hair.

My old friend, Colin, who's emigrated from a Welsh farm to devote his life to mixing cocktails and even writing about them in magazines like Travel and Leisure, *shoots me a smile and starts mixing my drink without asking for my order.*

"And how is the writing progressing today, Chase?" he asks while carefully placing cubes of ice into a tall glass with silver tongs. "Or are we still recovering from sandhogging in those nasty, arid foothills?"

Looking up, I see the many photos of Papa Hemingway that adorn the cherry wood paneled walls. Papa battling marlin, shooting pheasant, drinking martinis in this very bar during the Paris liberation of '44, flirting with adoring women and, of course, typing away at his beloved Remington portable. How is it he made everything that's hard in life, look so easy?

"Little of both, Col," I say. "I don't know what's harder, beating my head against a Turkish rock ceiling or beating it against a typewriter."

He places the worth-every-penny twenty euro drink before me. "This will help cheer things up a little." Leaning in to me, whispering for my ears only. "And kill the nasty little black bug up your arse."

The woman turns to me, then peers at me with hypnotic green eyes.

"Now there's something you don't witness every day," she says. "A man who gets to hang around beautiful Paris and still find reason to complain."

My face fills with the red blood of embarrassment. Stealing a swallow of the cold, effervescent, lemon-lime, champagne and vodka-laced drink, my outlook suddenly turns optimistic once more.

"You're absolutely right," I say. "My apologies for bitching on this beautiful day in the city of lights. Trust me, I'm not normally this charming."

She holds out her hand.

"Elizabeth," she says.

She's wearing a lightweight linen shirt and the open sleeve gently glides down her forearm to her elbow when she lifts her hand. She's also wearing a half-dozen silver bracelets that jingle musically when they collide with one another.

I take the hand in mine, feel its softness, smallness, and warmth. I also notice her calluses. For as beautiful and put together as she is, this girl is no stranger to getting her hands dirty. Take it from one who knows.

"Chase," I say out the corner of my mouth. "Chase Baker."

"This is Elizabeth's first trip to Paris," Colin says while wiping out a glass with a white bar rag. "And since you, the local Renaissance Man, are also a licensed tour guide, I thought perhaps you'd like to show her around a little. That is your license is good in Paris." The wink that follows is so subtle, I come very close to missing it altogether.

"You asking or telling?"

She sets her hand on my forearm. "Now I'm totally embarrassed. You're probably way too busy, Mr. Baker."

"I just might be way too expensive. And please, call me Chase. Mr. Baker was my dad."

"Money's no object," she says with a wink. "Us anthropologists just pick it off the trees on our college campuses back Stateside."

"Anthropologist," I say. "So you are not just Elizabeth, but Dr. Elizabeth."

"Academically speaking."

"Tenured?"

"My own corner office, a key to the faculty lounge, and unlimited access to the copier and fax machines."

"In that case, you're on."

I feel her fingers on my arm, inhale her rose-petal scent. For certain, she's younger than me. Maybe even by ten years. But that doesn't seem to matter. All I know is that I'm immediately attracted to her. And *perhaps our meeting inside the Paris Ritz bar could be considered mystic karma at work.*

"What time shall I pick you up tomorrow?" I say, stealing another generous sip of my '76er. "And where?"

She relays the name of her hotel and what time she'll be ready.

"Pleasure to meet you, Doc," I say, finishing my drink.

"Pleasure's all mine," she replies. Then, "And, Colin, it's quite the pleasure being served by a master drink mixer and matchmaker."

"Pleasure's all Mr. Baker's." He smiles.

Exiting the bar, I feel slightly tipsy, but also lighter than air. Like a teenager who just asked a girl to the prom...a beautiful girl who said Yes.

The next day is bright, pleasant, and not overly warm, even for summer, as if God has personally scripted it for us. I meet her at the Place de la Concord end of the Tuileries and together we walk the gravel footpaths that separate the green gardens, slowly revealing little tidbits about our lives. Me, the man with too many jobs...the sandhog, the private detective, the walking tour guide, and the novelist. Also the man who is divorced.

"Happily, I assume," she says, not without a giggle.

"Yes, happily. But I'm not happy about missing out on much of my daughter's upbringing."

"And the Renaissance man is a dad, too," she says as we pass by a fountain spouting streams of water into a circular pool that looks inviting enough to swim in. "Will the surprises never cease?"

Her, the anthropologist, was born and schooled in Philadelphia by a middle-class Irish Catholic family who thought she was nuts for spending as much time as she did in India, Nepal, and other parts of the world that she described as "difficult." She's thirty-four years of age and never had time for marriage, not to mention children, but looks forward to the day when some little rug rat is running around the house, calling out "Mommy" every few seconds.

But before all that, she's committed to locating the Golden Kali Statue. Nothing will stop her from finding it. And as she reveals the diamond-encrusted statue key from where it hangs around her neck by a thick leather strap, she insists she's close to locating it. Closer than she used to be anyway.

"I can feel it in my bones," she adds for emphasis.

Her enthusiasm is contagious even for an old sandhog like myself.

"When you're done, you can write a book about your experiences, do the talk-show circuit and be famous. You won't even remember who I am."

"Very funny. Science isn't about fame, Chase Baker. It's about discovering the past and learning a little more about why we exist and how much longer we have to exist."

"That's deep," I say, to which she responds with a gentle punch to my left bicep. The love tap sends chills up and down my backbone.

Sometime later, she reveals that her only claim to fame is her big advertising executive brother who created a global campaign for a Mexican beer featuring a handsome white-bearded gentleman who claims himself as The World's Most Interesting Man.

"Come to think of it," she says, as we share ice cream cones while watching the little French kids ride the carousel, "you're that man...the most interesting man in the world."

"You should live with me for a while," I say, taking

a lick of the sweet vanilla ice cream. "You'd be bored out of your skull."

Her green eyes take on a sheen that reflects the sunlight shining down on Paris. I just want to jump into the pools, swim around inside them for a while, then float on down to her heart, take a long nap. Without asking, she takes hold of my hand, presses her lips together. She says, "Maybe I'll take you up on that."

We spend the remainder of the day looking at paintings in the Louvre, then walk the Seine while fishermen angle for black, eel-like fish with their extra-long poles. We share a picnic lunch of red wine, cheese, sausage, and baguette and lie on our backs facing the sun. I've only been acquainted with Elizabeth for a few collective hours and already I feel like I've known her for years and years. After a time, I roll onto my side, place my hand on hers, lean in to her, and kiss her gently on the mouth. Much to my delight, she doesn't pull away, much less slap me.

"That was nice," she says when finally we come up for air. "You fancy yourself a tough guy, Chase Baker. But deep down, you really are a romantic."

"I live in my own little world," I say, kissing her once more. "I like it that way. But then, maybe you can be a part of it." Pressing my hand against my heart. "There's room enough for both of us in here."

"Does that mean I don't have to pay for the tour?" she says, giggling.

Night arrives gently after a brilliant orange-red sunset that reflects off the still river. We share a dinner of steak-frit and a bottle of expensive red while on a riverboat cruise that sails up and down the Seine. We retire to my room at the Saint James Hotel on Avenue de Rivoli and make love like we invented it. In truth, I expect her to be gone the next morning, already on a *plane bound for New Delhi. But when I wake up, I'm ecstatic to find her standing by the open French doors wearing a thick white robe. She's holding a cup of coffee in both her cupped hands while peering out at the view of old Paris, the Eifel Tower so clear and prominent in the background, it seems like she can simply reach out and touch it.*

"Come back to bed, Elizabeth."

She turns to me, issues me a pout that makes me want to melt into the mattress.

"Chase," she says, tears pooling in her eyes. "Do you believe in love at first sight?"

"I do," I say. "We're proof."

"I love you," she says. "I...love...you."

The Kali statue was Elizabeth's passion and obsession. As hard as I fell for her, I knew that inevitably I would be in for a world of hurt if I fell too far. You see, she was too much like me. If opposites did indeed attract, we were naturally doomed. She was simply too involved with her work. But then, work wasn't the right word for it. She was more like a shaman or a saint who had given herself over entirely to another power far greater than the mortal sum of all her parts.

Still, the trap door had been opened and not only did I fall for her, I kept on falling. And when she left me for good, I forced myself to not think about her. To forget her entirely. Because remembering her face, her voice, her smooth skin, her hair...was all too painful. Maybe that's why I never went after her. Because I was afraid of being hurt again. Afraid of her leaving me again. But then, I guess you could say, even after all this time...even after convincing myself that she was dead...I still love her with all my heart.

When we come to number 69 Via Guelfa, I unlock the front door, flip the light switch in the dark corridor. Climbing the short, but steep and narrow, flight of damp stone stairs to my apartment, I let us both in through the thick wood door. Almost immediately we're greeted by my five-year-old pit bull, Lulu. Lu takes one look at the tall, turban wearing man and growls.

Some people are deathly afraid of pit bulls. But Dr. Singh displays not an ounce of fear. He slowly lowers himself down to one knee like he did in the Piazza Santa Maria Novella, and gently holds out the back of his hand. Lu takes a quick whiff of it and starts to lick the hand as if he's fallen under the Indian's spell.

Singh stands. "When you are gifted with such a beautiful animal, life is never lonely."

"Man's bestest buddy. Do anything for you. He's also one hell of a guard."

I'm reminded of Lu saving my life in this very apartment not too long ago, back when I was in search of the mortal remains of Christ and some crooked cops from the Florence police wanted the prize for themselves.

I instruct Dr. Singh to make himself at home in the living room while I cross over the dining room into the kitchen where I put on a pot of water for tea. In the meantime, I crack myself a Moretti beer in hope that the buzz I had going an hour or so ago might quickly return bringing along with it the calming of my still beating, but no less broken, heart. When the tea is done, I pour a mug and bring it and the beer out with me into the living room.

"You've read all those books?" he says, nodding at

the floor-to-ceiling bookshelves that cover the exposed brick wall in the near century-old apartment building.

"If I'm not writing, I like to be reading. But nothing replaces seeing things for yourself. Traveling, getting the feel of a place. Smelling the smells, tasting the flavors, touching the textures. I'm sure you know the drill, Doctor."

"You speak the truth," he says, taking the tea in hand, nodding his head in thanks, then, exhaling. "I suppose you want to know how I'm convinced your Elizabeth lives and how I've become aware of her whereabouts."

...You're Elizabeth...

I steal a drink of beer, feel my heart beating inside my ribcage. "First of all, Dr. Singh, you must have done your homework to know that I experienced a love affair once upon a time with a woman named Dr. Elizabeth Flynn. And second, if you've spent that much time doing your homework, you must be jonesin' to employ me."

"Jonesing?"

"Figure of speech."

"Ahh, yes." He beams. "Now I remember...Back when I was in college, students would *jones* for a cigarette. Or some marijuana. Or some Old Milwaukee beer. Very bad for the digestive track."

"Exactly."

"I can't reveal precisely who my sources inside India and Nepal are. But word has come to me that Elizabeth Flynn is indeed alive and located somewhere near the Chitwan National Forest along with my son."

"She and Rajesh are together?"

"Yes." He swallows hard, his Adam's apple

running up and down the interior of his neck. "The search for Rajesh is all-consuming, Mr. Baker. And I can't think of a better man to get him back for me...for his parents. Therefore, I have indeed done my research and what I found along the way might startle you."

"And, of course, you're not going to give me any details about Elizabeth's so-called resurrection until I locate Rajesh and bring him back to you."

"You use the word resurrection, Mr. Baker. But are you certain she perished in the first place?"

In my head, I travel back five years.

I'm pacing the wood floor of my apartment, worried out of my skull because I haven't heard from Elizabeth in close to a month. Of course, it's possible this is her way of ending it, but my gut tells me different. A call comes on my cell phone. One of those calls that have a certain ring to it. A ring that signals anything but the garden variety phone call. A ring that instead stops your heart, sends a shot of ice water through your veins. I answer the phone, put it to my ear.

"Yes," the word peels itself from the back of my dry-as-sand throat.

"Are you Chase?" speaks the voice of a woman on the other end. "Chase Baker?"

"I am."

"My name is Samantha. I'm calling from India. I'm a colleague of Elizabeth Flynn's. I'm...I'm afraid I have some bad news for you..."

Dr. Singh is right.

Elizabeth was never reported as perished. Officially, that is. But what her colleague revealed was that she'd gone missing in Nepal, somewhere near the Chitwan National Forest. That the Nepalese Army was looking for her, but coming up with nothing. I can't begin to tell you how many times I nearly dropped everything to go look for her. But something stopped me. A voice inside me that kept telling me Elizabeth didn't want to be found. And that if I did succeed in finding her without getting myself killed, she'd just leave me again...or worse, send me away.

That was half a decade ago, just weeks after my father died of a heart attack. Since that time, I haven't heard a word. Until last month that is, when I received a strange envelope in the mail that contained no return address. Inside the envelope was the bronze key she'd discovered in the Rome antiquities shop...the key to the Golden Kali Statue...along with a letter.

The letter, which contained only a few words and a couple of hand-drawn but detailed illustrations of the statue, was signed by Elizabeth. Up until I pulled that letter out, I didn't know whether or not to take the key seriously, as if it were an elaborate joke cooked up by some sick-minded individual.

But then, this was no ruse. It looked very much like the real thing. A totally legitimate letter signed by the woman I loved but tried so hard to forget. Maybe at the time I should have been happy to receive some proof of life, but that proof only made me more confused and even more despondent.

"No, Dr. Singh," I say, choosing not to reveal any news of the bronze key or Elizabeth's letter to him. "I never saw her in death. Only in life."

"Then, perhaps resurrection isn't the correct term. But all this is simply semantics. The important thing is that if you agree to help me, I can lead you to her, Mr. Baker. In fact, your locating her will be a crucial component of the project."

"If locating her is the same as locating Rajesh,

why not go after them both yourself? Why bring me into it?"

"Too many eyes are already upon me. I'm afraid if word were to get out about my personally searching for Rajesh, his life could be immediately terminated. It's a risk I cannot take. Which is why I am asking you to go after him in my stead."

I drink some more beer to dislodge the distaste in my throat. Pulling the beer away from my lips, I toss it across the room, lunge at Singh, grab him by his jacket collar.

"Why are you doing this? Why not just ask me if I'd like to help? What the hell kind of head game are you playing, Doc?"

Lu barks, stands four square on the floor like she's about to bite Dr. Singh's kneecaps off should I issue the order.

"Back off, Lu. This one's mine."

"Mr. Baker, enough," he pleads, his voice raised a decibel or two. "Please understand, I have nothing directly to do with Elizabeth Flynn's life or death. I have made no direct contact with her. I only know what my information sources relay to me. That you were once lovers and that she lives and that I am someone who can provide you with at least some information that could potentially lead you to her whereabouts."

I let him go and he brings both hands to his throat as he seats himself down onto the couch.

"That makes my day complete. If she's alive, like you say, then you're using her whereabouts as leverage? What kind of man are you?"

"I want Rajesh back, Mr. Baker. Simply asking you for your services is not enough. Money won't be enough. Not even a lot of it. I need the utmost assurance that you will indeed find the boy and bring him back to me, no matter the cost."

"You're not taking any chances on me saying no, are you, Doc?"

"You might not have known Elizabeth for very long, but I am assuming you loved her with all your heart. Her capture is, in a way, my good fortune. Rajesh's good fortune. His karma at work."

...His karma...what about my karma, pal?

"Love...Love is why I'm saying yes to going after your six-armed God Boy."

"Love...Is there no better reason on earth for saving a soul touched by God?"

Dr. Iqbal Lamba Singh stands, reaches into his jacket pocket, pulls out a considerable wad of Euros. "Take this. Consider it a down payment. You will be hearing from my associate within the hour regarding the information you'll need to know prior to proceeding with the assignment."

"Not at this address. You've already revealed that the eyes of someone or something are upon you. For all I know, you're being followed right now."

"Then, I will make certain to have the associate available to you at your home away from home. The Fiddler's Elbow."

"That will do just fine."

"One hour. I should warn you that you are to leave tonight."

"You don't waste time, Singh. What about weapons?"

"Something to defend yourself with should the situation get dangerous?"

"I'm strictly offense."

"It will be taken care of." Handing me the cash. "Remember, one hour."

"How will I get a hold of you if I should suddenly require your assistance? You know, if I should happen to step into some quicksand or something?"

"I will be in touch. But don't worry. There's little chance of you stepping into quicksand where you're going. Everything has been arranged, or will be arranged. Do we have an understanding?"

"You knew I would agree to the job. Once you mentioned Elizabeth. You never even asked about my fee."

"Your fee is of no concern. It will be paid if you succeed and, by all means, the down payment is all yours no matter what."

"What if I don't succeed?"

"But you will. Soon you will find Elizabeth."

"But this isn't really about her is it? It's about the six-armed boy."

"It is about the boy. You see, Mr. Baker, locate Elizabeth Flynn, and she will lead you directly to Rajesh. Now do you understand my logic?"

"I do. And conversely, if I find the boy first, it's possible he might lead me to Elizabeth."

"Perhaps that is equally true. But in all likelihood, Elizabeth will be out in the open, working on uncovering the mine, while the boy will be hidden away in a chamber or a cell, separated from all who seek a glance at him and, shall we call it, his condition."

"One more thing, Doc. Who the hell took Elizabeth and Rajesh in the first place?"

He shakes his head and gestures with hands as if

to say, *not now*. "That will all be explained to you. Suffice to say...a man of extreme evil."

The devil...he's talking about the fucking devil.

I see the doctor out, lock the door behind me. Reaching inside my T-shirt, I pull out the leather strap wrapped around my neck and twirl the small bronze key it supports in my hand, the tiny diamond fragments embedded inside it sparkling even in the dimly lit apartment.

Slipping the key back inside my shirt, I then pull out my wallet, open it, slip my fingers into one of the slots, pull out a photo. Stare at the image. Elizabeth's face. She's smiling, a smile that crinkles her green eyes as her long hair blows in the breeze by the cobbled riverbank in Paris. I feel my throat tighten, my eyes well up. I knew the moment I met her in the Ritz Bar that I would marry her someday. But that day never came because Elizabeth disappeared and...died.

Or did she?

Lulu trots out of the bedroom, stares up at me.

"What the hell am I doing? I've finally gone and lost my marbles, Lu."

"For starters," the pit bull says, *"you're talking to a dog."*

"I'm not really talking to a dog. I'm only *imagining* myself talking to a dog."

"Okay, whatever. But something's got you upset."

"You think it's possible for somebody to come back from the dead, Lu?"

"Only in story books, Chase. Isn't that one of your many jobs? To write stories? Fantasies? Adventures?"

"I guess. They seem real when I'm writing them."

"Well, there you go. There's nothing wrong with suspending your disbelief now and again, especially when it comes to someone you miss so much."

The dog turns tail, hops up onto the couch, rests her chin on her front paws, falls to sleep.

"Have a good nap, Lu. Looks like I'm not going to get a lot of sleep tonight, so, I think I'll do the same."

Heading into the bedroom, I lie on my back, close my eyes. Within minutes, I find myself drifting until the drifting becomes a deep sleep.

I see fire. I am down in a pit or a cavern. A portion of the floor flows with a river of lava. It's so hot I can hardly catch my breath. Sweat leaks from my pores as if my skin were a sieve. Then, something begins rising from out of the lava. First, a head. Then, a set of arms, and another, and another. Soon the entire body has risen out of the hot flow and hovers above as though levitating.

It's the God Boy.

He locks eyes with me as I step towards him, only to feel myself sinking into the lava. But then, I'm not really sinking so much as melting into it. The pain is beyond anything I've ever felt.

The God Boy reaches out with all six hands.

"Touch me," he says, in his soft voice, "and you shall be healed."

I wake up in a pool of sweat.

It's as if the temperature in Florence has risen by one hundred degrees. I slide off the bed exhausted, make my way across the length of the apartment to the bathroom, stare into a cracked mirror at my distorted face, the crack making it look like my skull has been fractured vertically down its center. The face peering back at me is withdrawn, eyes red, scruffy covered skin, pale and sallow. Maybe it's the result of having spent most of the afternoon drinking. But then, it could be something else. It could be that already the God Boy is affecting me. Getting under my skin. Touching my soul.

I wash my face, dry it, avoid any further contact with the stranger in the broken mirror.

Out in the living room, I dig into the left chest pocket of my bush jacket and produce the letter that came with the bronze key one month ago...to the day I realize. Peering down at the page, I view a hand-drawn illustration of an eight-armed Kali holding what appears to be shrunken hearts in the palms of six of her hands while with the seventh she holds a sword and in the eighth, a severed head that's still alive.

The full frontal illustration is accompanied by an equally detailed one of the statue's backside. There's an area of the upper back that's been boxed out in pencil. Inside the box is written one word in big capital letters: KEY. Below that are written the words:

Chase, they are coming for me. The evil ones. Do not lose this key. It's all that separates my life from certain death. I never stopped loving you.

Elizabeth

Once more, I open my wallet, slide out her photo, peer into Elizabeth's green eyes. I feel their power as if she were standing right before me in my apartment. Again, I pull the bronze key out of my shirt, feel the solid object in my hand. I can only wonder if it's the true Kali key. And if that is the case, what secrets will the statue reveal once unlocked?

"Are...you...alive?" I say at the photo as if expecting an answer.

Returning the letter to my shirt pocket and the photo to my wallet, I grab my shoulder-holstered Colt .45 where it hangs on the wall-mounted hat-rack, slip it on over my shoulders. Then, grabbing my leather jacket from the hook beside it, I slip that on. I pull the automatic from the holster, thumb the clip release, make a check the nine-round load. Cocking one into the chamber, I engage the safety and return the piece to its resting space beneath my left arm, grip inverted for easy access.

"I'll be back, Lu."

Unlocking the deadbolt, I open the door and exit the apartment, the pit in my stomach telling me that although my new assignment to find the God Boy has yet to begin, I'm already in way too deep.

ARRIVAL AT THE ELBOW.

Part of me thinks it would be hilarious to enter through the window I was tossed out of just this afternoon. But I'm not feeling very entertaining right now. I'd rather cry than bust a gut. And anyway, a team of blue-overalled workers are busy installing a new picture window in place of the one that was shattered by my rather compact, but solid, five-foot nine-inch, one hundred eighty-five pound frame.

As usual, Matt is behind the bar still wearing his ABCD, AC/DC black cotton tee.

"No more trouble, Chase," he says, popping the top on a green bottle of Heineken for me. "You're costing me a small fortune in glass. Not to mention the words 'Fiddlers' and 'Elbow' I'll need to have stenciled on it. You know how much one of those artists charge?" He says "artist" like "*arteest.*"

"Don't tell me, Matty," I say, grabbing the beer, taking a quick swig. "Tell Joe muscles over there. And we're in Florence for God's sakes. Everywhere you turn you see a starving *arteest*. Make a trade for crisps and beer."

Matt purses his lips, crosses sinewy arms, concealing the ABCD on his T-shirt as if seriously contemplating the idea.

Four stools down, Calum is busy staring at his smartphone while working on a pint. I approach him.

"Yo, Cal." Reaching into my pocket, retrieving not the thick wad that Dr. Singh gave me, but the far thinner one I grabbed earlier. "I believe this belongs to you."

Matt races over, snatches the Euros off the bar.

"You mean, they belong to *me.*"

Reaching into my pocket, I pull out the big wad, slip off three five hundred euro notes.

"This cover it, Matt?"

He gives me bug eyes.

"That'll do nicely," he says, in his Irish brogue. "It'll cover the beer too."

"Good. Then give Calum back his cash."

Calum, sets down his phone, takes a hit off his pint, holds out his sledgehammer of a hand. "No hard feelings, Chase. Don't know me own temper sometimes. Plus, that man in the funny turban...the way he looked at me with his eyes. Made me feel real bad for tossing you out the window, even if you did deserve it."

"That's why our necks won't allow us to look backward." I shake the iron-gripped hand. Then, look around the sparsely populated bar. "Say, Matt, you didn't happen to see a stranger walk in a few minutes ago."

"It's Florence, Chase," Matt says trying to imitate my New York accent. "Just about everyone who walks in here is a tourist which makes them a stranger."

Peering around the long, narrow bar room, I make out a couple of college-age kids drinking pints of Guinness. Also a tall, dark man standing at the far corner of the bar. He's sporting a trim, salt and pepper beard. For a split second, I believe I've found my man.

But then, I take notice of the person seated a few stools up from him—a woman. She's on the small side, if not petite, but sporting a shapely body packaged in a short black skirt, a white button-down shirt that's unbuttoned just enough to reveal a pair of fine breasts supported by a black pushup bra, and gladiator sandals. Her black, shoulder length hair is lush and parted neatly above her left eye. She's typing on an iPad while sipping Prosecco from a long-stemmed glass.

Calum drinks another swig of beer, wipes his mouth with the back of his hand. He glances over at the woman, then back to me.

"Not bad, huh?" he says under his breath. "She breezed in about fifteen minutes ago, set up shop right there. Wonder if she's single."

As if sensing the subject of our conversation, she turns and gives me a look with these wide, dark eyes and equally dark brows that are as mesmerizing as they are attractive. When she smiles at me, I know I've found my contact. After all, Dr. Singh never specified a gender when he informed me about making contact with his associate.

"Excuse me, gentlemen. Looks like I have a date."

Grabbing my beer off the bar, I step over to the woman. "Saving this stool for someone?"

She looks up, smiles a sultry smile. "It is reserved for you, Chase Baker."

Her accent is not Italian, nor is it English, but something more exotic. Asian if I have to guess.

Judging by the rich, coffee with milk color of her skin, maybe Indian or Pakistani.

"Where you from?"

"My mother is from Pakistan. My father is from India. I was born in Varanasi. Made for a complex relationship, two sworn enemies defying their parents, marrying for love anyway."

"What's your name?"

She holds out her hand.

"I'm Anjali," she says.

I take hold of the small, warm hand. Give it a gentle squeeze. Releasing it, I sit myself down, steal another sip of beer.

"Dr. Singh said you'd have some information for me."

"Is there a place we can go that's more private? I'd rather not discuss details in front of your pals."

Like boss, like employee...Secrecy is essential.

In my head, I picture the Ponte Vecchio. It's not nearly as packed full of tourists at night as it is during the day.

"I know just the place."

Packing up her iPad, she shoves it into her leather bag, drinks down the rest of her Prosecco, slides off the stool.

"Lead the way, Mr. Baker."

My first full view of her take-no-prisoners body. Outstanding. Maybe this job won't be so bad after all.

"Call me, Chase."

On our way out of the bar, I shoot a wink at Calum and Matt.

"Some guys have all the luck," Calum says loud enough for me to overhear. "Or maybe my karma just sucks."

"You might think twice next time about who you're tossing out a window," Matt says.

WE WALK OUT OF PIAZZA SANTA MARIA NOVELLA
down a narrow road that leads directly to the river.
Maybe two hundred feet on the right is the Ponte
Vecchio, one of only two bridges spared by the Nazis
when they blew them sky high to prevent the allied
advance during World War II. The old iron lamps
mounted to the bridge's stone buttresses illuminate
the now cool, foggy evening in inverted arcs of smoky
lamp light.

When I come to the mid-point of the bridge—an
open area sandwiched between the many butcher-
shops-turned-jewelry-stores—I stop, turn, and pull the
.45 from my shoulder holster.

Anjali's dark eyes go wide. "What are you doing,
Chase?"

"What's happening here? Your boss just happens

to know a little bit too much about my life. Knows where to find me, knows about my past loves. Or love, anyway. Why do I get the feeling that finding his God Boy is a do or die mission? As in, I either do it, or die."

She feigns a smile. "You have Dr. Singh all wrong, Chase. Finding Rajesh is his number one priority and he knows you are the only man in the world capable of that task."

"That why he tossed in the little bonus about Elizabeth Flynn? My heart tells me she's dead, Anjali. But he claims she's alive."

"Dr. Singh might be many things, but a liar is not one of them. If he knows of this Elizabeth you speak of and he says she is alive, then you must believe him."

"He claims to be a psychoanalyst or clinical psychology professor or both. But tell me, what's Singh's real business?"

"He has many businesses. His family has gathered great wealth and prestige over the decades. He is an investor. He is also a generous benefactor. One of his passions is children. The new children's hospital in New Delhi was personally financed by him. Rajesh is his son. It has not been easy for him, having to bear the burden of a child with six arms."

"Okay, he's got a lot of dough and he's nice, and he's got a lot of college degrees to prove how much smarter he is than me. But why insist on messing with my head? That one of his little psychoanalysis tricks?"

She eyes the gun barrel. "Pardon me for saying so, but I'm not sure it's your head he's messing with. Perhaps your heart would be more accurate."

I exhale, lower the gun, return it to the holster.

"Show me what I need to know, Anjali."

She digs into her bag, retrieves the iPad, fires it up. The screen illuminates with a man's face. It's covered with a thick, black beard, his eyes shielded by aviator sunglasses. His hair is equally black, his skin dark like an Indian or perhaps even a man originating from one of the Stans...Pakistan or Afghanistan. I can't see precisely what he's wearing, but judging from his shoulders and collar, he's sporting a military-style tunic.

"Do you know this man, Chase?"

I stare at the face. It isn't the least bit friendly.

"Can't say I know the man," I say truthfully. "But the more I look at it, the more my mind spins."

"His name is Ilyas Kashmiri and, until recently, he was the head of Al Qaeda's 313 Brigade."

My pulse picks up. Bingo. Now I recognize him.

"I know of 313. They're the terrorist team that operates out of Afghanistan and Pakistan."

"Exactly. They also have ties to the Iranian-backed Hezbollah, and more recently to ISIS regiments both in Syria and Iraq. They are cold-hearted killers and they have spilled much innocent blood in the name of Allah."

"What's this got to do with a boy born with three sets of arms?"

"Radical Islamists, especially those belonging to ISIS, wish for one thing: world war. A jihad to end all jihads. A war that will unleash Armageddon for which they will gladly die. That happens, the sky will be filled with martyrs all making their way to heaven..."

"...And their forty virgins...I'm already well aware of this bedtime story, Anjali."

"Kashmiri and his 313 believe with all their hearts that it is just a matter of time until enough atrocities against Christians, Jews, Westerners, and peaceful Muslims occur, and that the United States and its allies will have no choice but to commit to a total war against Radical Islam and all its differing factions, including 313."

"Here's what I believe," I interrupt. "If that kind of global war were to occur, it would not last very long. Would you like to know why?"

"Why, Chase?"

"Because evil bastards like Kashmiri will die and die quickly. ISIS, 313, Al Qaeda, and all of them lack an important tool for waging World War III. They haven't got the money to unleash a world war. No heavy armor, no heavy assault weapons, no Air Force, no Navy...need I go on? The most they're capable of are lone wolf attacks outside the Stans, Africa, and the Middle East. They also lack unification. As much as they fight the West, they also fight and kill one another."

"You don't need to go on, Chase, but your point is very well taken, which leads me to why Kashmiri is interested in Rajesh. You see, the terrorist has set his sights on something far larger than 313 or ISIS. He wishes to unite all the differing terrorist factions in an unholy axis of evil by resurrecting the ancient Thuggee cult."

The hair on the back of my neck pricks up. "The original terrorists. Responsible for millions of innocent deaths. Until the British wiped the cult out. I've already discussed this craziness with Singh."

"There are people today who believe ISIS and Al Qaeda are Hell incarnate on Earth, just like the Indian Sikhs and Hindus of yesteryear believed the Thuggee was Satan on earth. The Thuggees were believed to maintain a very real and special relationship with the evil God Kali herself. Kashmiri would require a special power to raise the Thuggee from the dead. A direct connection to Kali."

In my head, I recall Dr. Singh describing Rajesh's miracles.

"The kid," I say.

"Rajesh is a special boy. A God Boy, as you called him. A healer. A miracle maker. To men like Kashmiri, he is a direct link to God or…" Her voice trails off.

I turn to her, peer at the lamp light reflected in her dark eyes.

"Or the Devil," she adds. "You see, Chase, like the black Goddess Kali, Rajesh can be utilized for both good and evil purposes, just like a mortal man, who himself is capable of both good and wicked."

My stomach drops. "I think I see what's happening now. Kashmiri kidnaps Rajesh, believes he can use the kid to summon up the power of Kali and the evil Thuggee. With the power of the devil behind him…"

"His new Thuggee army of terrorists, formerly aligned with Allah, now becomes invincible. However, it still needs one thing more."

"And that is?"

"Funds. Enough cash to build an army bigger than that of the United States of America."

I stare out over the river. It's black and haunting. The way it flows beneath me makes me feel lonely and cold even in the warm weather.

Anjali flips through more digital pages on her iPad until she comes to one that shows a gold statue—a photo I instantly recognize as the eight-armed Goddess Kali.

"Several weeks ago, our spies intercepted an email intended for officials at Rhode Island's Providence College in the US. It came from a scientist digging beyond the boundaries of the Chitwan National Forest in Nepal. It reads: *'Kali Statue located. More beautiful than believed. She rests upon a blue rock that shines with brilliance. Fear I won't live long enough to examine her for the secrets she possesses.'"*

I lock eyes on her iPad. I see the words printed digitally on the electronic page, but they don't register entirely. Like a sickness that has only just surfaced inside my gut, I pause to await the onslaught of pain. Pulse pounding, mouth dry, I feel the solid weight of the bronze key wrapped around my neck and I recall Elizabeth's letter. In my head I read the words, *"...I'm already dead."* Is it possible the letter and the email originated from the same woman?

"This Golden Kali Statue means something to you?"

"Of course it does. The statue has been buried for centuries. Hidden. Up until now, it was the stuff of legend. Fantasy. Treasure buried where X marks the spot or some such nonsense."

"Lots of ancient statues of Kali have been buried and unearthed."

"Yes, but this one is special because of a map it contains. It's also believed to contain something of special spiritual significance. Don't you see?"

She shakes her head.

"Listen," I say, recalling my many conversations with Elizabeth over just what the Kali map might lead to. "If the email is correct, then someone has discovered the one map on Earth that could lead directly to the Daundia Khera."

"The massive diamond deposit?" Anjali questions.

"Exactly. A big, brilliant, blue rock. The story goes that back in the early part of the twentieth century a holy man named Swami Shobhan Sarkar experienced a vivid dream one night. He dreamed that a Thuggee rebel by the name of Ram Baksh Singh came to visit him. Singh had been dead since 1857 when he was hanged by the British government for his participation in the Thuggee uprising. But, in the dream, he is said to reveal the exact location not of the diamond deposit itself, but instead, the map of the deposit's location. That map is believed to be printed on the back of the Golden Kali Statue."

"And you believe now that this email indicates the map has finally been found?"

"Maybe what it means is that the Kali Statue isn't a map at all but, instead, a marker that indicates the precise location of the Daundia Khera."

"Why do you say that, Chase?"

"If Kashmiri wants to summon the devil, I'm guessing he believes the God Boy can do it. He also needs the funds to build an army like no one has seen. That diamond deposit, if found, contains more precious gems that any other mine on Earth. If uncovered, the Thuggees won't have to worry about buying tanks because they'll be able to afford every rogue nuclear weapon on the planet and the delivery systems capable of attacking every city in Israel and the US. It would trigger the end of times."

"There's something else. That diamond deposit is said to contain unearthly powers. If unearthed it would summon a thousand devils."

"And Rajesh? What happens to the kid if we don't find him?"

She looks into my eyes. "In my mind, Rajesh is to serve as the sacrificial lamb."

"They're going to kill him?"

"If they sacrifice such a special, spiritual boy in the name of Kali, Rajesh will be immediately reincarnated into something so wicked no one will be able to stop him. The Thuggees will have their evil leader and they will have their nuclear arsenal. They will conquer anything or anyone they want." She steals a moment to breathe. "The world will belong to Satan...to the Thuggee...to the new terrorists."

We both stare at the river for a beat.

"We should go," Anjali says.

"Yeah, we should. But answer me one question. That email about the Kali statue. From whom did it originate?"

"Do you really need for me to say it, Chase?"

"Yes," I say, hearing the sound of the name even before she speaks it.

"A woman by the name of Dr. Elizabeth Flynn," she says.

Just the sound of her name causes my bones to shudder. A cesspool of emotions well up and boil over. But it all makes sense to me now. Kashmiri must have found out about Elizabeth's work in Nepal near the Chitwan forest where she disappeared five years ago. When he discovered she was close to uncovering the Golden Kali Statue, he had his bandits move in and abduct her. With Elizabeth, and now the God Boy, in his possession, his plan to unleash Hell on Earth could be completed.

"What about you?" I ask. What's your stake in this, besides playing the role of dutiful employee?"

Anjali stops, turns to me, the lamplight glowing in her now damp eyes.

"Rajesh is my son."

A **PRIVATE JET WAITS FOR US AT THE AEROPORTO DI**
Firenze-Peretola. Having run back to my apartment to
change into a pair of cargo pants, a tan work shirt,
Chippewa work boots for footwear, and my worn-in
bush jacket (pockets stuffed with everything from
passport to a mini first aid kit), Anjali and I are
escorted to the runway via private van. Once aboard
the jet, we're greeted by a pilot who smiles and shakes
my hand with all the eagerness and enthusiasm of a
professional politician.

"Welcome aboard, Mr. Chase Baker," the Indian
man greets me. "I've heard much about your exploits."

"I hope you still respect me," I say. Then, "What,
no copilot?"

"God is my copilot." He laughs, then introduces us
to a female flight attendant whom he calls Beatrice.

She's tall, tan, with dark hair cropped short, and a tiny green jade stud pierced into her perfect nose. Her outfit is a dark blue miniskirt and matching jacket, a pair of gold wings pinned to her lapel.

"Once airborne, she will serve you drinks and dinner," the pilot adds. "Now, please, take your seats and buckle up. We're about to take off." Reaching, he pats my side. "Oh, and Mr. Baker, I am going to have to ask you to surrender your weapon for the flight."

I shoot Anjali a look. She nods. "Don't worry. You'll get it back when we land."

Reluctantly, I pull the automatic from its shoulder holster, hand it to the pilot.

"Thank you for your cooperation, Chase," he says, heading back into the cockpit.

Anjali and I head to the passenger section, take two of the six available seats, she on the port side of the aircraft and I on the starboard side. Beatrice brings us champagne and offers a choice of meat or fish for dinner. I choose beef while Anjali goes with the fish. Maybe we can share. Chase the hopeful and the hungry.

Questions float around my brain like stars. Are Anjali and Singh still married? Singh told me he's been living in the States for the past five years. Why did he leave his wife and his boy? Did he leave them out of shame? How, exactly, did Rajesh get kidnaped? Why does Anjali seem to have no fear over partnering up with me in going after her son while Dr. Singh says it's too dangerous...that too many eyes are on him? Whose eyes?

Once airborne, I've barely consumed my first glass of champagne when I begin to feel sleepy. Unusually sleepy. But then, it's past midnight and the nap I took earlier didn't really cut it. Renaissance men like me need their beauty rest.

Stealing a quick peek at the very quiet Anjali, I can see that her eyes are closed and that she's caught up in a deep sleep. She's snoring ever so lightly, her left hand still wrapped around her drink which rests on her foldout tray.

That's when I decide, *What the hell. I'll close my eyes for a few minutes until it's chow time.*

I fall immediately into a cavernous sleep. *And that's when she comes to me.*

Elizabeth, with her long, strawberry blonde hair, standing beside me at the train station in Varanasi. It's five years ago, but it's also right now. Right this very second. We're holding hands, but our palms are cold and perspiring. Not because we are so in love, but because we've reached a crossroads. Elizabeth, the archeologist obsessed with uncovering the Golden Kali Statue, and I, the sandhog wanting her to forget about the impossibility of ever finding it. Wanting her to come with me to New Delhi, and from there, back to the US to be married, start a family of our own.

We are surrounded by people. So many people it's as if there's not enough oxygen to go around. Hordes of Indian travelers dressed in colorful tunics. Some men proudly sport the turban of the Sheik. Others wear nothing on their heads. Women with long, black hair veiling their faces, a perfect circle tattooed in the center of their forehead. Exotic and alluring.

The trains come and go at the busy station, the smell of locomotive exhaust tainting the air, carriages covered with the men and women who either can't afford to ride inside or just can't find the room. Old men peddle hot peanuts while small, impossibly thin, young boys jump down onto the tracks as soon as the trains pull out. Their sole objective is to collect the used clear plastic water bottles which they will then fill with common tap water, passing the cholera-tainted poison off to unsuspecting tourists as fresh spring water.

I turn to Elizabeth, kiss her on the cheek, squeeze her hand. She looks up at me, brushes back her hair, allows it to rest on her white T-shirted shoulder.

"Do you love me?"

"You know how much I do," she says. "If anything should happen to me, just remember how much I will always love you."

"What on God's earth can happen to you, honey?"

"Just promise me you won't forget."

Then, something happens that breaks my heart. A single tear drops from her eye.

The train arrives in a loud cacophony of metal wheels against rails, high-pitched whistles, and a thunderous locomotive engine. When it comes to a stop, the air brakes hiss and spit smoke.

Grabbing my heavy pack off the concrete platform, I throw it over my shoulder.

"This is it!" Heading for the train as the doors open and the arriving Indians pour out of the first class cars. "Our new life begins now."

Without thinking, I enter the car while checking our tickets for our berth number. In India, if you don't grab your space immediately, someone else will snatch it up and it will be hell trying to dislodge them from it. Opening the door, I toss my bag onto the first class full-length seat that will also serve as a bed when nightfall comes. About-facing, I go to grab hold of Elizabeth's pack. But she's not standing there.

Leaning my head out the door into the narrow corridor, I search for her. She is nowhere to be found. There are only the Indian people filing into the car with all the steady intensity of the sand that pours into an hour glass. The atmosphere is at once chaotic but *somehow organized. The first whistle, indicating that the train is about to pull out, echoes through the train station.*

"Elizabeth! Elizabeth!"

Another whistle. The trains here don't wait for anyone. Too many people to transport. Not enough rail cars to accommodate them all. Not enough time.

Too...many...people...

I turn, go to the window.

There's a wave of people still struggling to board the train. I'm looking for Elizabeth, trying to pick her out of the crowd. I look for her khaki cargo pants, hiking boots, T-shirt, her hair held in place by a red bandana, the bronze and diamond-studded Kali key strung around her neck by the thick leather strap—she should be easily visible. But there are simply too many people.

Taking a step back, I open the door once more, push myself out into the corridor. But it's an impossible dream with the many men, women, and children trying to get through with their bags and luggage. The train begins to move. I feel the initial bucking, followed by the forward motion.

I go back to the berth, back to the window. As the crowd disperses, I suddenly see her, standing in the exact spot where I left her on the platform. Her arms crossed over her chest, her green eyes glowing and filled with tears. I try to pull up the window, but it's stuck.

"Elizabeth!" The train begins to move along the rails, leaving the platform slowly behind. "Elizabeth...!"

It's no use. She didn't miss the train by accident, or because of the onrush of people. She did it on purpose. She's going back to Nepal. Going back to dig for the Golden Kali Statue.

As the train begins to pick up speed, I place my

right hand on the glass of the window as my eyes fill with tears. I am helpless, the loneliness settling into my sternum like a rock.

"Elizabeth..."

Raising her right hand to her mouth, she blows me a gentle kiss.

The train moves faster now and just like that, she is gone along with the station. Vanished into nothing, but engraved in my brain.

My love is gone.

In my heart, I know I will never see her again...

Then...a bang and the aircraft shudders.

Sleepy eyes go wide. Peering over my left shoulder, I see something that takes a long moment to register. Precisely because, it's something I should *not* be seeing at thirty-three thousand feet above sea level.

The pilot with his hands wrapped around Anjali's throat.

SHAKE THE COBWEBS OUT OF MY HEAD. IT DOESN'T
take an Einstein to know that someone slipped a
mickey into my drink. That someone being the
friendly flight attendant.

"O' Kali!" The pilot is shouting. "O' Kali mother!"

There's something going on with his eyes. They
are wide, unblinking, and glowing, like an energy
from within is being released. A bad energy. A wicked
energy. Just the sight of them steals my breath away.

Slipping my hand inside my jacket for my .45, it's
not there. Pilot took it off of me earlier. I could dig
through my jacket pocket for my Swiss Army Knife,
but no time for that. Instead, I dump my drink, crack it
against the edge of a solid plastic and faux wood tray,
breaking the glass to form a crude knife. A swift kick
knocks it out of my hand.

Raising my head, I see Beatrice staring me down, her body having taken on the offensive posture of a black belt. Her eyes have gone just as wide as the pilot's, the whites glowing with rage. Is it possible I'm caught up in a Tarantino movie and just don't know it?

Raising my hands, I try to reason. "I'm sure we can work something out, Bruce Lee."

Before I have the chance to register her left leg coming up, she swift kicks me in the jaw with a right foot saddled in a black pump. I fall back, my head slamming against the port-hole window. Groggy, I shake my head.

"Does this mean the dinner service is discontinued?"

Reaching into her jacket, she pulls out a knife. A twelve-inch fighting knife to be precise. Something an ISIS assassin would brandish on the internet.

"Kill her now," she barks to the pilot. "In the name of Kali, slice her throat."

The pilot produces an identical knife from an ankle sheath, brings it to Anjali's throat. Maybe it's the sharpness of the blade pressed up against the soft skin that wakes her. But her eyes suddenly open.

"You bastard!" she screams, bringing her right knee up swift and hard, nailing the pilot in the sweet spot. Not even his evil eyes can protect him from a swift kick to the balls.

He shrieks, pulls the knife away.

Beatrice comes after me with her own knife, but I shift myself forward at the last possible moment. She lands in the seat on her face and chest. Grabbing hold of her arm, I pull it behind her back, bending it in a way God did not intend. The knife drops from her hand, falls onto the seat. I pick it up, jump across the aisle, and bury the blade into the pilot's ribcage.

He drops on the spot.

"Chase!" Anjali shrieks.

Turning, I spot a pistol barrel staring me down. My own pistol poised in the hand of Beatrice, our not-so-friendly, bright-eyed flight attendant.

"Duck!"

The shot singes my hair as it blows out the window next to Anjali's seat. The abrupt change in air pressure sends the pilotless plane into a nose dive. It also begins to pull us, along with the pilot's body, towards the gaping hole, as if an angry God himself has gripped us in a pair of invisible hands.

"Hang on," I shout while feeling for Anjali's seatbelt, buckling it around her waist, pulling the strap as tight as it will go without cutting into her stomach.

She fires again, but she's out of balance and another hole appears above the busted out porthole. At first the hole is small. About the size of my fist. But the force of the escaping air is shredding the plastic and metal fuselage. That's when the dead pilot's body lifts off the seat, his head and shoulder pressed into an ever-widening hole that is joining with the shot-out window to form one big, man-sized opening. For a brief second, I consider grabbing hold of his legs. But he's already dead. A second later, the pilot is sucked out of the hole and making his way back down to Earth the hard way.

But now, it's my turn to get sucked out of the opening.

My legs lift up off the floor. I'm being yanked out of the plane right behind the dead pilot. Not exactly the way I pictured my inevitable demise, preferring instead to drift off to sleep in my ripe old age and never wake up.

Beatrice fires again and another hole appears beside the big one. I'm holding on to the metal frame beneath Anjali's seat, double-fisted. The plane screams as it speeds towards the earth like a missile. Peering over my left shoulder, I see the flight attendant floating towards the opening. She, too, is being sucked out. My pistol still gripped in her hand, her face painted with panic, she tosses the automatic out the hole while attempting to grab ahold of something. Anything.

...*Christ, there goes my gun*...

"Please...help...me!" she screams. But her words are barely audible with air rushing in and the plane in rapid decent.

She begins to claw at the seats while her entire body lifts up, the powerful vacuum-like suction pulling her head-first out the opening. Glancing over my shoulder through the breach in the fuselage, I watch her limbs waving and kicking spastically as she enters into a three-mile drop without a chute.

...*Don't let the door slap you in the ass on the way out*...

Looking up, I see the look of desperation on Anjali's face.

"Don't worry. I'll get us out of this."

But unless she can read lips, she has no clue what I'm saying.

Choices: I can either continue to hold onto the seat and ride this bird to the ground in which case we'll be vaporized by the crash, or, I can make my way to the pilot's cabin, hand-over-fist, and attempt to level her out at an altitude and speed that will cut down on the exterior air pressure.

Easy peasy, right?

Problem is, I'm not a pilot. But I have to at least try.

Pulling myself into the aisle, I grab onto my seat. That's when something catches my eye. The rear lavatory door. It's blown open. Stuffed inside the cramped compartment, seated on the toilet, are two people—both of them duct-taped together.

It's the rightful pilot of this aircraft and his flight attendant. Chase Baker the charmed.

A WAVE OF WARM OPTIMISM FILLS MY VEINS. I CAN only hope the pilot is still alive. And if he is alive, I hope he's conscious enough to pull us out of this dive. Quickly, I make my way the ten or so feet to the lavatory, crawling on my stomach for the entire distance. For some reason, if I crawl, the suction is not so bad. When I look up, I can see the pilot's eyes are wide open. So are the flight attendant's. Also, their whites aren't glowing or burning red or turning anything other than their natural, God-given color. More good news. Raising myself up, I pull the tape off his mouth.

"You the real pilot?"

"Cut me loose," he shouts while alarms blare from inside the cockpit. "Do it now. We're dropping three thousand feet per minute. Three minutes before this thing careens into the Arabian Sea."

Reaching into my jacket, I find my Swiss Army knife, flip open the big blade. Pressing the business end of the blade on the tape that binds his wrists together, I cut. While he pulls his hands apart, I reach down and cut the ankles. Without issuing a single word, the pilot drops down to all fours, begins speed crabbing his way to the cockpit.

Meanwhile, I pull away the tape that gags the flight attendant and free both her wrists and ankles.

"Thank you," she says, mouthing the words.

I take her by the hand, pull her along with me to one of the free seats. She slips into it, securing herself with the belt.

"Buckle in," she insists.

"I'm going to keep the pilot company," I insist, crawling my way to the cockpit, stealing a quick glance at Anjali along the way. She's shivering in the cold. Still, she issues me a forced smile, but I know she's not happy. "Now's a good time to pray," I yell to her, but she can't hear me over the blast of air pouring in through the opening.

Once I reach the cockpit, I slip myself into the co-pilot's chair. By the look of the altimeter, we've got about ten thousand feet left to work with.

"Strap yourself in," says the pilot. "Things could get a bit shaky."

I do it. "Shaky's fine by me. So long as we live to feel it."

He pulls back on the yoke. The plane bucks and bounces, the engines scream in protest. The G's we're pulling are so intense, my stomach feels like it's about to spill out of my feet. But after a few seconds, the plane levels out then slowly starts taking on altitude.

"With that hole in the fuselage, the pressurization

is shot," the pilot says. "We'll fly her up to twenty thousand for the duration."

"You mean you're going to take us to Nepal as planned." A question.

"Those are my orders. We're alive. The plane flies, and the bad guys are gone."

I reach out with my right hand. "Chase Baker. Damn glad to know you."

He grips the hand tightly, gives it a shake, releases it.

"I'm not entirely sure what you're after, Mr. Baker. But it must be important to attract that kind of trash onto this plane."

"You mind my asking who they were?"

"Radicals," he says. "Hindi terrorists. Thuggees. Vermin who have promised their souls to Satan and who distort the evil half of Kali for their own selfish purposes. Warped people who do not want you to succeed in your mission."

I'm reminded of what Anjali revealed about Kashmiri and his dream of an evil Utopia utilizing Dr. Singh's six-armed kid. Surely the bad guys would be opposed to our mission to stop them. But, what's really upsetting is that they already know about the mission.

"Please don't take this the wrong way, Captain..."

"Mumbai. Like the city."

"Captain Mumbai. Why'd they let you live?"

"Same reason you wanted me to live. To land this plane. That terrorist was capable of taking off. But landing was a different story entirely."

"Guess they felt the same way about the flight attendant."

"They would have kidnaped her in the end had they succeeded, sold her into slavery. She would bring a nice price on the terrorist black market."

"Nice bunch of people operating in the name of Kali these days," I say, my tone full of acid.

"You don't know the half of it," he responds. Then, "Two hours more until we reach Kathmandu. Go on back and try to get some rest. The hole is no longer a danger now that the pressure has been equalized, but it's cold. The attendant will hand you a blanket."

"If you don't mind, I'll stay right here and enjoy the view."

He laughs.

"Please do, Mr. Baker," he says. "By all means, sit back, relax, and enjoy the flight."

WE RIDE IN AN OPEN-TOPPED JEEP FROM THE SMALL
airport into the heart of Kathmandu. The city is as hot
as it is congested and smog-filled. The narrow streets
can barely accommodate the mix of old and young,
dark, leather-skinned natives dressed in bright saris
and robes. Cars made in China spit black exhaust
while drivers pound the horn and curse to their
Hindu, Muslim, and/or Christian Gods for the crowds
to move out of their way or else be run down. On both
sides of the street, ancient Hindu temples are filled
with worshippers while small fires burn in clay bowls
and monkeys use the tall minaret style architecture as
if they were trees in the forest.

The temples are surrounded by three and four-
story ancient wood buildings that look as if you can
blow them down with the gentlest of exhales. Besides

natives, the streets and sidewalks provide access to all varieties of animals—including cows—who seem to enjoy the right of way. We pass by a team of young adventurers carrying ropes and climbing boots strung around their shoulders. They wait impatiently for their number to come up in the Everest climbing lottery. That is, if their number comes up at all. Just a couple of months ago a team of Sherpas were killed in an avalanche that also took the lives of the Italian climbers who employed them. Since then, the Sherpas have been on strike, leaving the climbers frustrated with not much else to do but roam the ancient streets.

But, at least Kathmandu is known as much for its monkey-filled temples as it is its bars. One glance upwards and you can't help but notice the revelers who lean out the windows of the many drinking establishments, Nepal Ice Beer bottles in hand. With marijuana and hash being as free here as the wind, this is a place where hippies traveled to en masse in the 1960s for spiritual enlightenment and a good buzz. Many of them OD'd, but many survived, thrived, and never bothered to go back home.

The Jeep finally makes it to the gates of the Kathmandu Guest House, the oldest and most famous of the Kathmandu inns. Or so the old driver informs us.

"This is where George Harrison, the Beatle, stayed," he proudly states while retrieving Anjali's bags and my shoulder bag. "Here, he wrote many, many songs."

Inside the lobby of a nineteenth-century wood and stone structure that looks like it was lifted from an old English garden and resettled here, we are handed the keys to two rooms, both of which adjoin.

At the top of the stairs, we open the door to my

room and step inside. That's when we see that an interior door separates my room from Anjali's. She shoots me a smile and a wink over her shoulder like I had planned it this way all along.

"Hey, you're the one who made the reservations," I say. "So, don't blame me."

"I'm going to freshen up," she says. "I'll assume this door will be locked."

As she exits the room, I reach over to the inside door, unlock it.

"Oh, it'll stay locked."

I make out her laughter as she enters her room. Chase the devious.

I go to work right away, pulling my computer from my shoulder bag, booting it up. I look up the name Elizabeth Flynn in a Google search, just as I've done a thousand times since we parted at the Varanasi train station. Naturally, I come up with nothing. No Facebook or Twitter accounts. No LinkedIn. Nothing. There's maybe a dozen Elizabeth Flynn's out there and a dozen more with variations on the given name (Betsy, Liz, etc.), but not my Elizabeth and certainly not one residing in Nepal. It's as if she disappeared off the face of the earth five years ago. Something not all that difficult to do in a mostly forested and mountainous country where the majority of residents outside of Kathmandu don't even enjoy the benefits of modern electricity much less internet access.

Closing the lid on the laptop, I stand, pull Elizabeth's letter from my jacket pocket, set it on the laptop. I begin to unfold it. But then something holds me back. There's this pit in my stomach that tells me I'm not only beginning to believe that Elizabeth is alive, but that it's possible we'll somehow pick up where we left off.

69

That's insane.

Even if she is alive, she made it clear that our relationship was over, no matter how much we loved one another. My job right now is to find Rajesh. If I can manage to locate Elizabeth first, she might show me the way to the God Boy. That is, if she isn't already dead. But then, if she is alive, she'll have quite a bit to answer for. Like not ever picking up the phone for five years to let me know she's not dead.

Suddenly, all the pain of those many nights not knowing where she was, if she were alive or dead, or even in the arms of another man, starts coming back to me. Maybe she entrusted me with the Kali Key and a letter containing an illustration of her most prized obsession, but that doesn't take the place of her being my lover and partner.

Christ, I was willing to settle down with her. Marry her. Have children with her. That's not something that comes easy for me. But she didn't want it, and now, here I am feeling like a giddy school kid just back from summer vacation, dying to get a look at the girl I had a crush on all last year.

I toss the letter down onto my laptop.

"Screw this. Maybe I'll be able to locate the kid without having to run into Elizabeth."

Picking up the phone, I call the front desk. When the concierge answers, I ask for a bottle of champagne to be sent up to my room.

"Right away, sir," he says.

"Oh and be sure to put it on Dr. Singh's tab."

"Of course, sir. Will there be anything else?"

It dawns on me that I haven't eaten in almost twenty-four hours, especially after our in-flight meal was so rudely interrupted. I tell him to also bring up an early lunch. Traditional Nepalese would be fine.

"And plenty of naan," I add.

"Of course. Thank you, sir."

I hang up, slip my bush jacket off, roll up the sleeves of my work shirt, lean my shoulder against the fireplace mantle. I imagine a nattily mustached British Colonel in leather riding boots and epaulets pinned to his shoulders doing the same thing a century ago, back when this guest house served as a British headquarters for their colonial armies. I know I should set my emotions aside and get back to work on locating Elizabeth. But truth is, I'm also wondering what Anjali is doing next door. If she's asleep in her bed. If she's naked or clothed or merely just wearing a pair of panties. Nice little black lace ones. One detail I was quick to notice earlier was the absence of a wedding band. I know she's Rajesh's mom, but my guess is she's no longer married to my boss, Dr. Singh.

It's tough to think on an empty stomach.

Moments later, the doorbell rings.

Opening the door, I'm happy to see that the wait staff has wasted no time in delivering the food and champagne. I'm just about to have the boy set the stuff on the bed when something devilish dawns on me.

"I have a better idea," I say, stuffing three hundred Nepalese rupees in the boy's white-jacketed pocket. I tell him to take the order next door, compliments of Mr. Chase Baker.

"A beautiful lady stays in that room?" he says with a smile.

"Yes. A beautiful lady indeed."

"Oh," he says, the soft cheeks on his tan, young face blushing. "I see."

"Yes, you see. Now go."

He gives me a look like we both share a man-to-man secret and because of it, we're now blood brothers. He goes next door, rings the doorbell. Closing my door gently, I then place my ear to the interior door. I make out some shuffling about, then the exterior door opening.

"Oh my," Anjali says, "I don't recall ordering lunch...and champagne too."

"Compliments of Mr. Baker."

I hear the door close. Suddenly I feel my heart beating just a little bit faster than it was five minutes ago. I head into the bathroom, look at myself in the mirror. Running the water, I wash my face and attempt to straighten out my short hair as best I can for someone whose hairline is receding faster than the Red Sea for Moses. Then, satisfied that my appearance isn't going to get much better any time soon, I make my way back across the room, set my left hand on the knob of the interior door while wrapping with my knuckles on the door panel with my right. Twisting the knob, I open the door just enough to poke my head inside.

"Are we decent?" I say. Spotting the food and champagne set out on the bed, I open the door wider. "What's that, lunch?"

Anjali is kneeling beside the bed, her hands folded in prayer. She's wearing nothing but a thick white towel with the Kathmandu Guest House logo printed on the breast pocket.

"Really, Chase Baker," she says after a beat, looking up at me with her deep brown eyes. "What if I were kneeling here entirely naked?"

"If wishes were fishes," I say. "We'd all have a fry."

"What's that mean?" She smiles.

"I'm not sure. My mother used to tell me that every time I wished for a new toy." Then, "Hey, you're praying just like my mother taught me how to pray. Hands pressed together and everything."

"Are you surprised to see that I am a Christian...a Roman Catholic...and a devout one at that, Chase?"

"Not at all. Millions of Catholics in Pakistan, India, and Nepal."

She stands, slides onto the bed. "Now," she says, smiling slyly while softly patting the empty space beside her on the mattress, "you mentioned something about a toy. Is that what I am to you, Chase? A new toy?"

"Right now, it looks like you're lunch, and I thought you were a devout Catholic."

"I'm also a big girl who is free to do what she chooses with the gifts God gave her."

"And how does my employer, Dr. Singh feel about that?"

"We divorced not long after Rajesh was born. He left the country, moved to New York."

So it's true...she is divorced...

"Too bad," I say, praying that the smile trying to form on my face isn't noticeable.

I step into the room, slowly make my way to the bed, setting myself down beside her, resting my back against the soft, down pillow. The sumptuous lunch is laid out before us.

"Would you care to join me, Chase?"

"If wishes were fishes, boss lady," I say, bringing my arm around her, pulling her to me, my lips meeting hers.

12

"So much for maintaining the boundaries of the sacred employer-to-employee relationship," Anjali says through a sly but attractive smile while sipping on her second glass of champagne. "But then, I'm not really your boss, am I?"

We're both sitting up in bed, the metal pans of food devoured along with most of the champagne.

"Shall I call down for another bottle?"

"Or we can get some work done, lover," Anjali says, feeling for my hand under the covers, giving it a squeeze. "Any ideas about finding your ex?"

Shaking my head. "I'm still trying to wrap my head around the fact that she might still be alive. Took me quite a while to get over her."

Anjali snickers. "This proves it," she says, referring to our little late morning interlude. But then, her light moment suddenly takes on an air of substantial heaviness. "Perhaps you feel it wrong of me to think of making love at a time like this...when my only child is in danger."

"I'm no judge of that."

"This here...you and I enjoying one another's bodies for a brief moment...it is also a kind of defense mechanism. Something to keep us, or myself anyway, from imagining the worst." She looks away. "Sometimes I need to stop my mind from working, churning up bad thoughts of Rajesh."

I nod. "It's not all that different for me. If I were to allow my imagination to take over and truly get used to the idea of Elizabeth being alive...the possibilities...it could be heartbreaking in the end."

"Yes, because what if she is alive, and she rejects you once more?"

"Like I said. I'd rather not think about it."

She gently fingers the bronze key hanging from my neck. "What's this? Or am I not supposed to ask?"

I explain its presence and the letter that arrived along with it only last month.

"Proof at last that Elizabeth lives," she adds.

"Possibly. But if Elizabeth happens to be alive and we do find her, it will be strictly business. After all, what kind of woman doesn't contact you for years, even if she did send me a key that quite possibly unlocks the secrets to one of the most sought out statues in the world? What kind of person does something like that?"

Squeezing my hand again. "Perhaps a selfish woman who doesn't love you any longer. But also a woman who, at the same time, still trusts you. Obviously, she doesn't want the key getting into Kashmiri's hands and there's only one person in the world who can make sure of that."

Her words make my stomach hurt. Or perhaps it's all the Nepalese delights. But then, she's right. If Elizabeth truly loved me, she would not have allowed me to go on believing she was dead for as long as she did. That's cruel. It's one thing to put one's career over one's love life, but it's another thing altogether to compound the pain of separation by feigning death. But then, did she really feign death? Or did I just want to believe she was dead?

"If she's out there, Chase," Anjali goes on, "we need to find her. She's our direct link to the Kali Statue, the location of the diamond deposit, Kashmiri and, most importantly, Rajesh."

"It's likely we'll find all of the above at the same time. But, you're right. For now, the most logical person to seek out is Elizabeth. If I were Kashmiri, I'd keep the boy hidden inside a cell or a box or somewhere no one can get to him. He is precious cargo. More precious than the diamonds. Elizabeth, on the other hand, she will be found out in the open, digging, searching, proving her usefulness to Kashmiri until she can prove it no longer. But where to start looking? That's the ten million dollar question."

Coming from outside, loud rapid-fire explosions. My senses perk up.

"What's that?" Anjali poses, panic in her voice. "It sounds like gunfire."

"Calm down." Slipping out of bed, I head for the window in my birthday suit. "That's not gunfire. That's a sound I've been listening to all my life. It's a ninety-pound jackhammer." Pulling back the curtain on the picture window. Outside in the Kathmandu Guest House courtyard, a crew of construction workers are chewing up the existing concrete sidewalk with a jackhammer and a JVC excavator. That's when it hits me over head.

"Excavators," I say.

"Excuse me?"

Turning.

"Excavators. It's possible we might find Elizabeth's location from an excavator....a digger. They're an essential part of any archeological dig. I should know. I used to be one of them. Only we didn't call ourselves excavators. We called ourselves sandhogs."

"Sandhogs," she repeats like I've just said something entirely foreign. "But there must be a thousand diggers and excavators and *sandhogs*, as you call them, in Nepal. What are the chances of us finding the one man who knows where Elizabeth Flynn is presently unearthing the Golden Kali Statue?"

Returning to the bed, I sit down on the mattress, start putting on my clothes.

"I think I know a man who can help."

"You don't sound very encouraged—or enthused—by the thought."

"That's because I'm not very enthused by the idea of contacting him. But he's our best bet if we want to find Elizabeth."

Biting down on my bottom lip, sighing.

"Why so glum?" Anjali asks.

"The man I'm speaking of used to work for my dad's excavating business. When my dad died, he wanted to keep the business going since it was his livelihood. But I shut it down to devote to my writing career full time...my adventures. He never forgave me."

"But he's here in Nepal?"

"Last I heard, he's in Kathmandu, working for the university archeological teams that are constantly moving through here and northern India."

"What's his name?"

"Anthony Casale...he was born in Italy. Naples. He moved to Brooklyn when he was still just a boy." I slip on my work boots, turn and smile at her. "A bit of a hot head."

"All your friends are hotheads." She smirks. "They like to throw you out windows. Or, so I'm told."

"I tend to have that kind of impact on people."

"It's your charming personality. Do you know how to find Anthony?"

"Not precisely. But I know how to get started finding him."

"How?"

"We start at the first bar on one side of the city, then begin working our way to the opposite side of the city until we find him."

"Big drinker?"

"You have no idea."

"Well," she says, tossing off the sheet. "I am a bit thirsty after that spicy lunch."

My eyes lock on to her perfect naked posterior.

"Bottoms up, boss lady," I say.

13

THE PLAN FOR FINDING TONY IS MORE THAN JUST
looking for a toothpick inside a box of toothpicks...a
little more scientific than just taking a chance on
spotting him in any one of a thousand bars operating
inside Kathmandu. Back in my room, I retrieve
Elizabeth's suicide letter, stuff it into my pocket.
Then, lifting the computer lid, I Google Anthony
Casale Excavating. Thank Providence, or Brahma,
because unlike my experience when searching for
Elizabeth, not only do I get a website that advertises
his digging services, but I also get a map of his
shop's whereabouts.

Anjali comes up behind me, pulling her hair into a
ponytail when she peeks over my shoulder at the
Google map. She's wearing black jeans, black combat
boots with her pants tucked into them, and an olive

green blouse with pockets over both breasts, the tails hanging out.

"He's not far from here," I say. "We'll take a rickshaw."

She points to the map and the orange arrow that indicates the precise location of Casale Excavating. "Is that where we'll find him? In his office?"

"There's bound to be a bar next door or close by. *That's* where we'll find him. I guarantee it." I slip into my bush jacket, fold the sleeves up to my elbows. Raising my right hand, I pat the now empty space over my heart, and recall my .45 flying out of the hole in the plane. "Crap."

"What is it?" Anjali says.

"I forgot to look into a weapon. I...*we*...should have an equalizer or two now that word of our operation has reached the bad guys."

She grabs hold of my arm while biting down on her bottom lip.

"I almost forgot." She goes back into her room. When she returns, she's carrying a heavy-duty, plastic case which she sets on the bed.

"This was already in the room waiting for us when we got here, care of my ex-husband. I told you I would take care of everything you need for finding Rajesh."

I set my hands on the briefcase-like latches, thumb them open, lift the lid. There's a pistol pressed inside a foam holding core. A Colt .45 automatic and two additional clips. Also two stacks of cash laid out on top. Nepalese rupees and Indian rupees. All large denominations. The final item inside the box is a shoulder holster with elastic straps.

I pocket both stacks of cash, then remove the weapon and the clips.

"Nice work, boss lady. My preferred caliber, even."

Punching one of the clips into the stock, I pull back the slide, loading a round into the chamber. The second clip gets pocketed in the right-hand pocket of my jacket, easy access. Once again, slipping the jacket off, I fit the holster over my shoulders and store the Colt under my left arm, grip inverted. I pull the jacket back on, concealing the weapon entirely.

Back to the Google page and the address of Casale Excavating. Retrieving a pen and paper from the desk, I write the address down and stuff it in my pocket along with Elizabeth's letter.

"What about you, Anjali. You packing?"

She reaches around back, lifts up her blouse, produces a small caliber automatic. Also a Colt.

"That makes me feel better," I say. "We should go."

Going for the door, I open it.

"Chase," Anjali says before I step out.

I turn. "What is it?"

"What we did this afternoon...our lunch. Just so you know, I'm not going to hold you to anything." She inhales, exhales. "And if Elizabeth is alive..." Her sentence trails off. But her point is received loud and clear.

"I understand...two ships passing in the late morning far, far away from home."

Once again, she bites down on her bottom lip. I find myself doing the same thing.

I walk out.

IT TAKES THE RICKSHAW A FEW MINUTES TO
negotiate the busy downtown street to what serves as
the Casale Excavation Company. The sinewy driver,
who can't weigh more than one hundred fifteen
pounds, pedals with bare feet, the soles of which have
certainly turned to leather. He shoots and scoots in
between people, cattle, and taxi cabs, creating a plume
of dust in his wake. If we'd taken a car, it might have
cost us a half an hour to travel the same distance.

As predicted, located directly beside the Casale
office is a bar. Judging by the red neon mounted to
the interior of the establishment's front picture
window, the name of the joint is Rudy's New Orleans
Jazz Revival.

Catchy.

Dismounting the rickshaw, I pay the man double

what he asks for and immediately head to the front door of the bar, Anjali on my tail.

"Aren't you going to at least check the office first, Chase?"

"That's funny," I say, opening the wood door, stepping inside.

For a few seconds, I stand inside the old bar, soaking in the timber plank floor, its wood walls and dark, smoky interior. To my right is a large, stone fireplace. Even with the outside temperature close to eighty degrees, a small fire burns inside the hearth. To my left is a long bar. A man is seated at the far end of it. I know him like I would a brother. If I had a brother.

After a beat, the door opens again, and Anjali enters.

"Is that him?" she whispers.

"That's him. Watch yourself. He starts swinging, you'll be glad you kept your distance."

"Sounds like a real nice guy."

"He's a sandhog and an angry one at that. How much nicer can he get?"

The center of my chest goes tight. I begin to make my way towards the opposite end of the bar, my shadow growing on the wall behind Casale with each step I take, like a giant dark ghost.

"That's far enough, Baker," the short, muscle-bound, mustached man says in his Brooklyn-accented English.

"You call that a greeting, Tone?"

"I should have known that I'd run into you sooner than later. So, how's the writing going, Renaissance man? You famous yet? Was it worth putting me out of a career?"

"There was no business left to give you a career when Dad died. You know that. He *was* the business. I had no choice but to bury it along with his casket. Besides, judging from the sign out front on the joint next door, looks like you've done pretty well for yourself over here."

He chugs the rest of his beer, sets the bottle back down onto its condensation ring, wipes his mouth with the back of his meaty hand. "Who's the dame? You on your honeymoon? A pretty girl like that deserves a *Sandals* vacation in the Bahamas. Not this shit hole." Then, raising a hand to his mouth, as if to make a megaphone. "Run now honey, this one will bail as soon as he feels like it. Not a loyal vein in his body. Take it from one who knows."

My face fills with blood, heart pounds against my ribs like it wants to get out.

"Listen, Tony," I say, taking a couple of steps forward. "I know you don't like what happened with the business, but maybe we can help each other out now."

A short, beer-gutted man appears from behind a curtain that hangs over a door-sized opening behind the bar. The clean-shaven white man, who is definitely a westerner, smiles, attempts to straighten out his head full of salt and pepper hair, asks me if I'd like something to drink. But when he sees that Tony and I are not exactly locked in welcome embrace, his face tightens up.

"How about beers all around?" he suggests in a British accent. West London if I have to guess.

"That would be swell, Rudy," Tony says. "My friend Chase here is buying. Isn't that right, Chase?"

"But, Mr. Tony," Rudy says, "you own the bar now."

It takes some effort, but I manage to work up a grin. "Wow, a bar plus an excavating company. You must be doing better than well, Tone. Best thing that could have happened to you was my old man's business biting the dust."

"Yeah, I'm making a fortune. You looked at what the Nepalese rupee is worth against the dollar these days? So what do I have that you can possibly want?"

"Information."

"Regarding?"

"Elizabeth...Elizabeth—"

"—Flynn," he says in my stead. He takes on a smile. The same kind of smile he used to take on from up in the cockpit of a backhoe excavator when he would hit something solid and promising. Like the stone lid of a sarcophagus in Egypt or an underground tomb at the base of the Andes Mountains in Peru. Despite his thick hands and sausage fingers, Tony had the touch of an "angel," or so my dad used to say. He wasn't just an excavating operator. He was a magician.

"You still carrying a torch for that poor girl, Chase?" he says. "Not a very nice thing for your new lady to hear, especially when she's standing right behind you."

"Anjali," I say, "please meet Tony Casale. Tony, Anjali. And we are not what you think we are. We're business associates at present."

He lets loose with a belly laugh. If this were one of my novels, I'd describe the laugh as sardonic.

"Sure you are," he says. "But what the hell do you want from me? You come all this way just to ask me something? You could have called for that. Or texted."

He slips off the bar stool, stands. He tops out at maybe five feet six inches with his boots on, but with a thick neck, barrel chest, and hands as big as sledge hammers, he resembles a steel fireplug. A powerful fireplug. And damned if he doesn't know it.

I turn, shoot Anjali a look like, *well, so far so good.* Then, turning back to Tony, "I need some info on her whereabouts. Word on the street is that she's not dead…"

The punch comes from out of nowhere. I never saw the right hook coming. Suddenly, I'm down on my back on the bar room floor, bright white stars flying past my eyes.

"Chase!" Anjali shouts. She comes to me, helps me up into a sitting position.

"Happy?!" I say to Tony, rubbing the punch out of my jaw while climbing back up onto my feet.

"I've been waiting years to throw that punch," he says, massaging the now bruised knuckles on his punching hand. "I used to dream about it, day in and day out." Then, his happy face returning. "Yeah, I'd say I'm pretty fucking pleased with myself right now."

Rudy sets the beers on the bar. "Please, sir *and* sir, no fighting." He points to a sign mounted above the fireplace. It reads, "No Fighting!" in six or seven languages.

Commotion comes from behind me, and suddenly Anjali is handing me a beer, and then offering one to Tony.

"Let's calm things down, drink to something," she suggests. "To old times."

She raises her beer up as if to make a toast.

His eyes no longer glaring with hatred for me now that he's punched my lights out, Tony raises his beer up.

"What the hell," I say, raising mine.

Suddenly the phrase "O Kali!" is shouted out from across the vast room, and the beer bottle explodes in my face.

BULLETS SPRAY THE BAR.

We hit the floor.

"Who's shooting?" I bark, reaching for my new .45.

"That hooded son of a bitch at the door," Tony shouts. "Rudy. My piece."

With Anjali pressed against me, her little automatic in hand, I catch sight of the front door. There's a man standing in front of it. He's big, dressed in a black shin-length tunic, and a matching black hood. Only his dark eyes are exposed. He has a banana-clipped AK-47 gripped in both hands. Raising the weapon to his shoulder, he's striking a bead on our position on the dirty, wood plank floor. We're fucking turkeys inside a very shallow barrel.

I tip over the closest stool to create a barrier and fire off a burst which sends Black Hoody down to his knees.

Rudy stands. His own Kalashnikov gripped in his hands, he fires a short burst in the direction of the door, nailing Black Hoody in the chest. He then transfers a revolver down across the bar to Tony. The excavator grips the revolver and shoots at Black Hoody, hitting him in the thigh.

"That'll make sure he stays down," he says.

The picture window explodes and two more hooded gunmen jump through, Kalashnikovs blazing on full automatic.

"Other side of the bar!" Tony shouts.

We crawl as fast as possible around the wooden bar, bullets barely missing our heads and torsos, burying themselves into the thick wood panels. When all three of us are safely on the other side, I catch Tony's eyes.

"Did you bring these sons o' bitches with you?" he barks. "Thank Christ they can't shoot for shit."

More firing, directly into the bar, the bullets penetrating and nailing the bottles of booze stacked on the wall behind us.

"Chase, I'm not leaving this life without taking some of them with me," Anjali barks.

The woman's got spirit, I'll say that for her. Even if she is a devout believer in Jesus Christ.

"Look what they're doing to our bar, Anthony," Rudy laments.

"*My* fucking bar," Tony barks.

"I didn't invite them," I say. "But looks like they're crashing anyway."

That's when the grenade drops on the floor between myself and Tony. For a split second, we just stare down at the smoking grenade, like it's not real. Like what we're experiencing is a dream and we're about to wake up a split nano-second before this grenade explodes and tears our skins to shreds.

Instinct takes over.

Reaching for the grenade, I grab hold of it, toss it back over the bar in the direction of the front door. When it explodes, the bar shudders.

I stand, .45 poised before me, combat position. The hooded gunmen are down on the floor, bleeding out from mortal wounds. At the same time, the logs that were burning in the fireplace have rolled onto the alcohol-soaked floor. Several trails of flames are spidering their way along the rough wooden planks, up the wooden walls, and along the ceiling.

"Stay here," I say to Anjali, while going around the bar.

"Make sure those bastards are down," Tony insists.

The closer I come to them, I can see they're down all right. Down for good, as in, rest in peace.

The fire is quickly spreading throughout the old, dry wood structure.

"Time to abandon ship, Tony. This place is gonna flash."

He stands.

"Thanks," he says. "I haven't even finished paying off Rudy for the joint yet."

We all head for the front door which is wide open. We're not outside more than a minute when the entire place flashes over in a red hot plume of red-orange flame.

"Where are the police?" Anjali points out. "And no fire department?"

"Oh, they'll be here all right," Tony says. "In about an hour, as soon as they can manage to break through the traffic."

"Welcome to Kathmandu," Rudy smiles. "I hope you brought some cash with you, Mr. Baker."

"Who were those men exactly, Chase?" Tony says,

his face masked with both disappointment and anger. "And why were they barking about Kali when they busted into the bar trying to poke holes in my head?"

"Your garden variety follower of the evil Thuggee satanic cult."

"And why exactly are they trying to kill you and what does all this have to do with Elizabeth?" he says, as the burning timbers that support the roof of Rudy's cave in, sending shards of sparks out onto the street. Then, holding up his big hands in surrender. "Wait. Don't tell me yet. Put it all on hold while we find another place to talk before the friends of those satanic, militant whatchamacallits come looking for the roasted remains of their friends." Turning to Rudy. "Rudy, the truck please."

"Right away," insists the bartender, as he heads for the front door of Casale Excavating.

When he comes back around with a white Ford Expedition, the words Casale Excavating printed on the side, the L in Casale shaped like a backhoe bucket, we all pile in.

By the time we leave the scene, the Casale Excavating office has also caught fire.

16

WE HEAD BACK TO THE HOTEL AS QUICKLY AS HUMANLY possible through the congested streets. Upstairs, inside my room, we clean up. Then, with both Rudy and Tony seated on the bed, I explain our mission. I start with the abduction of Rajesh by the militant Islamist Pakistani, Kashmiri, and continue with his plan to resurrect the Thuggee cult. I explain about the lost diamond deposit and how Kashmiri will need it not only to fund his new evil army, but also to tap into its powers. That is, the legend about the diamond mine turns out to be true.

"That's where Elizabeth comes in," I say, standing by the front door. "I believe she's finally located the Golden Kali Statue. That would explain why she mailed the key to me along with the letter last month."

"So you think this Kashmiri jerkoff has been

holding her in captivity for at least a month?" Tony says. "And that she's still alive?" He reaches into his back jeans pocket, pulls out a round green can of chewing tobacco. Opening the lid, he pinches some of the sticky black tobacco and presses it between his cheek and gum.

"That's what I'm banking on. And if we find her, we find the boy and Kashmiri. What have you heard amongst the other diggers in Kathmandu, Tone?"

"Diamonds," Rudy interrupts, his round face beaming. "Did you say diamonds?"

"Last I checked, Rudy, I don't stutter."

Tony interjects, "Rumors mostly. That Elizabeth Flynn willingly entered into Nepal to dig for the Kali Statue. But that was some years ago. To my knowledge, she hasn't been heard of since. But, obviously. this Kashmiri character found out about her and set off after her."

"Five years ago?" I say, seeing her standing on the concrete train platform in Varanasi.

"Sounds about right," Tony confirms. "She went into the jungle five years ago. Not long after your old man kicked off."

"Ummmm precisely how many diamonds?" Rudy presses.

"More than the world has ever seen before in one single deposit," I say. "Or so legend has it."

"The Golden Kali Statue and the map it supposedly contains," Tony says. "That's just a myth. You know how many people have died searching for it? It's a fool errand. You of all people should know that, Chase. My guess is that Elizabeth has already died looking for it. Problem is, Kashmiri's found her. If she sent you that key, she must have been desperate enough to know he was going to end her life." Then, pointing to his tobacco-distended cheek. "Got something I can spit into?"

Looking over both shoulders, I head into the bathroom, grab the toothbrush glass, head back out and hand it to him. He spits a big wad of black goo into it.

"You should have quit that filthy habit by now, Tone," I say.

"Hey, some habits are tough to break," he insists like we're talking about heroin.

Anjali breaks in, "Dr. Singh believes the statue exists and that after years of digging, Elizabeth Flynn has indeed finally found it, and that she is alive. If his sources on the inside are correct, that is."

"So, if he has sources on the inside," Tony adds, "it's conceivable that some of the Thuggees are acting as double spies."

"The statue was her life's obsession," I say to no one in particular.

I pull Elizabeth's letter from my pocket, open it, hand it to Tony. He looks at the letter, reads it, studies the drawings for a moment.

"But once she was abducted by Kashmiri," he says, "she wouldn't be allowed to contact anyone on the outside. Least of all you. Somehow she managed it. But I guess he would want to keep her alive long enough not only to find the statue but, as the expert anthropologist, to have her reveal its secrets. And who knows how many secrets there remain to be revealed. I would not doubt she's very much alive if there's more mine yet to be discovered. She's too damned valuable as an expert on the statue, its secrets, and the mine it is attached to."

Locking eyes on Anjali. She doesn't have to speak a word for me to see the relief on her face. If Elizabeth lives because of her value, then there's an almost one hundred percent assurance that the God Boy would also be alive. After all, as the go-between for himself and Kali, the six-armed child is even more important than Elizabeth is to Kashmiri.

"Then you have an idea of Elizabeth's whereabouts?" I say.

"I think I know where to find her general location," Tony says. "She left Kathmandu with a group of archeologists who, at first, appeared to be legit. Sponsored by one of those Stan countries, I'm not sure which."

"Pakistan, more than likely. When was this exactly, Tone?"

"Back in 2010."

I recall my receipt of the letter and the bronze key a month ago.

"That would make sense," I say. "I'm going to go with the theory that she's being held against her will. Naturally, she assumed they would kill her once they located the Golden Kali Statue so she sent me the key. But maybe she's been finding excuses to stall Kashmiri all along."

"If she's smart," Tony says. "And if she values her life."

"If the map on the statue is there," I say, "it will lead them to the diamond deposit. That happens, there will be no stopping Kashmiri's new Thuggee army."

"It also means they will sacrifice Rajesh," Anjali says, clearly disturbed. She raises her right hand, looks up at the ceiling as though facing heaven and makes the sign of the cross. Then, "Can you lead us to Elizabeth, Mr. Casale? If we can get to her, she will reveal everything to us. She will know precisely where Rajesh is being held and how we can get to him."

Tony spits more tobacco juice into the cup, stands. The ever loyal Rudy also stands.

"I can try," Tony says. His eyes shifting mine "But it'll cost you, Baker. You of all people know I don't come cheap. Plus, there's the little issue of my burned up bar and my equally destroyed business."

I remember the wads of cash in my pocket. I reach in, pull out the stack of Nepalese rupees. I cut the stack in half, hand it to him.

"Down payment," I say. "I can get you the rest after I've located Elizabeth and the kid."

Rudy goes wide-eyed at the sight of the cash.

"In US dollars," Tony says, smoothing out his thick mustache with his thumb and index finger.

"Deal," I say. Then, "Now, show me what you know."

All four of us gather around my computer while, once more, I bring up Google Maps. I type in Chitwan National Forest and the entire one thousand square miles, rabbit-shaped wilderness appears. Tony takes a knee, stares at the map.

"You mind?" he says, setting his fingers on the keys.

"I don't recall you being fond of computers, Tone."

"People change, kid. When your old man died and my job was buried along with him, I was forced to learn a lot of new tricks."

We watch pensively as the veteran digger clicks away, focusing in on a specific plot of forest that's located all the way up to the northwest. An area of land that surrounds a town called, Dumkibas.

"According to what I've heard from some of the other diggers in Kathmandu who hang around the bar," he says, "your old girlfriend went into the woods somewhere around here before she disappeared."

Eying the cursor on the map. "That's not even in the park. Technically speaking. You ever been to Dumkibas?"

"It's just outside the park's northwest buffer zone," Tony says. "While the village is pretty densely populated with poor people living in tin and wood shacks, the town itself is a big nothing. A small street two-sided with a couple of bars and a general store of sorts. It's like the Wild West, only in Asia. It's surrounded by jungle that no one likes to enter because it's also home to some nasty elephant and rhino poachers. Other than the Nepalese Army, there are no cops, no sheriff."

Anjali elbows me.

"Jesus, Mary, and Joseph," she whispers. "Now we must deal with poachers in the Wild West."

"Not if we stay out of their way," I say. Eyes back on the map. "Can you be more specific, Tony?"

He shakes his head. "Wish I could. I only know what I've heard, and what I've heard is that she entered the jungle somewhere around Dumkibas."

"We gotta figure out a way to be more specific than that or it could take us weeks to find her in that thick stuff. By then she and the child could be dead. We just gotta hold out hope they haven't worn out their usefulness."

"I'm all up for ideas," Tony says, spitting one last wad of black tar into the glass, then taking it with him into the bathroom to deposit the used up tobacco in the toilet.

"Disgusting habit," I mumble as he flushes the toilet, washes out the toothbrush glass, and re-emerges from the bathroom.

"Perhaps we can visit one of the bars in Dumkibas," Rudy adds with a smile. "Surly the bartender will know of any strange women who've passed through the town."

"Not a bad idea," Anjali says. "That's how we located Tony."

"I agree," I say. "It's like Occam's Razor. The answer to our question is the simplest solution. But I'm afraid simple won't cut it this time. The bad guys are already onto us, which means time is already tight. We need to know Elizabeth's location right this minute. Not weeks from now, or even twenty-four hours from now. Like I keep saying, we find Elizabeth, we find the kid."

"Maybe *all* your focus on is Elizabeth," Anjali says, acid in her tone.

I turn quick. "Excuse me?"

"We're supposed to be focused on Rajesh. But since we've arrived all you speak about is Elizabeth."

I go to her.

"Look at me," I say, recalling our late morning lunch in bed, our lovemaking. "You either trust me and my decisions, or you find a way to fire me right now and I'll be on the first plane back to Florence. You got that?"

Truth is, however, I wouldn't leave. Not without Elizabeth or, at least, not without knowing the truth about her.

Anjali's eyes tear up. I wonder if she's also remembering our lunch and what she said about there being no real feelings attached to it. Of course, she was lying and we both knew it at the time, but refused to admit it.

"I'm...sorry," she whispers. "I just want my child back. So does Dr. Singh."

After a heavy pause, I take a mini-walk around the bed, then go back to the window, look out at the diggers still working on the sidewalk. They aren't using their jackhammers or excavators right now. Instead, a tracked skid steer is dumping gravel into a long trench while one man stands off to the side holding an aluminum pole that supports an electronic laser transit. Another man is holding what looks to be a remote control unit in both his hands while looking upwards at the blue sky behind Polaroid sunglasses. Following his lead, I too look up.

That's when I see the flying machine or, what's more commonly known in today's high tech world as a drone. The construction crew is using a drone and its GPS and infrared camera technologies to achieve the specified height for the new gravel they're installing.

I turn to the others. "I think I have the perfect solution to our time and Elizabeth location problem...a drone."

"A drone," Anjali repeats. "Like the unmanned airplanes Obama uses to kill terrorists within Pakistan?"

Shaking my head.

"No," I say, raising my hand. "The little propeller-operated jobs that construction crews, like the one outside this window right now, are using."

Everyone stands, gravitates to the window, and looks out at the airborne drone hovering over the hotel courtyard.

"Well, what do you know, chaps?" Rudy says. "It's like the model airplanes I used to fly as a kid back in merry old England."

"Tony," I say, "how difficult would it be to get us one of those, say, within the hour?"

"I know a guy who knows a guy," he says, turning away from the window, his eyes back on me.

"Won't the bad guys be able to spot the drone?" Anjali says. "Just like we spotted this one?"

"Affirmative," I say, "but by then, we'll be ready to make our move and snatch both Elizabeth and Rajesh from their grasp," I say this with a broad smile on my face as if it will be easy. Chase the optimist.

"And some diamonds," Rudy adds.

"Assuming she's alive," Anjali says.

"Like I keep saying," I repeat, "no time to lose. Tony, what time you got?"

"A little after one."

"Can we get the drone within the hour?"

He pulls his cell phone from his jeans pocket.

"Let me make some calls," he says.

"Meantime everyone, pack your bags," I say. "We're heading into the jungle."

TONY'S CALLS PROVE PRODUCTIVE.

His friend, who knows a friend, who knows a friend, leads us to the Kathmandu bazaar in the center of the city. It's a congested place with narrow alleyways that access old brick and wood buildings that house vendors selling everything from metal cookware to jade jewelry to pet monkeys. The place smells of peanuts roasted outside on small gas-fired stoves and, unless you know your way or follow someone who knows how to navigate the maze of alleys and corridors, you might get lost for days on end. It's that claustrophobic, that crowded, and that complicated to get around without a proper rudder.

When we come to a building that sports a glass façade displaying a sea of cell and smartphones, digital cameras, HDTVs, and all sorts of electronic junk, Tony turns to us, and barks, "This is it!"

We'd enter right away if not for the short procession of grieving men and women filing past. At the front of the procession, eight or so men shoulder a flat wooden platform that contains the body of a deceased man. The corpse is wrapped in a bright orange sheet covered in a colorful arrangement of flower petals. Soon, the body will be laid to rest on top of a large square platform of dried timbers that's been constructed on the riverbank. The wood will be set ablaze and the fire will consume the flesh and blood of the dead while the soul enters the body of another in utero fetus so that it might live again. Or so Hindu faith has it.

Walking through the front door of the shop is like entering another dimension altogether as the air conditioning cools our perspiring skin and the noise from the bazaar gives over to the sound of televisions tuned to stations broadcasting in several different languages. The man behind a long glass counter, that displays more of the same electronics, is big and burly. He wears a long green tunic, the sleeves of which are rolled up past his elbows. His hair is black and slicked back while his round face sports a thick mustache. The overhead ceiling fan blowing warm air down on him does little to stem the flow of sweat dripping from his forehead and armpits. He spots Tony and immediately breaks out into a salesman *Well-if-this-isn't- your-lucky-day* smile.

"And you must be Mr. Casale," he says in his amplified baritone. "Your cousin described you perfectly."

Turning to Tony. "Cousin?"

"Pays to have relatives living in Kathmandu," he whispers over his shoulder. "Even if you have to invent them."

While Anjali and Rudy hang back admiring the

television programs broadcast on a dozen different wall-mounted LCDs, Tony and I belly up to the counter.

"You were made aware of our needs?" Tony says to the man.

He smiles broadly, holds out his hand. "First, allow me to introduce myself. I am Bishal, and this is my humble shop of electronics, communications, and entertainment. A high-tech paradise like no other on Earth, this side of the Himalayas. I trust you will not be disappointed."

"That remains to be seen, Bishal," Tony says. "You have drones?"

The big man raises his hand, points an index finger to the sky. "The world of electronic gadgetry has adopted a new dimension. And, in keeping with Bishal's philosophy of cutting edge service, I am pleased to tell you that I not only have drones but several models in stock, right this very moment, at very affordable prices."

The big, perspiring man begins walking towards the back of the cramped store.

"Looks like we've come to the right place," I say to Tony. "Even if he does stink to high heaven."

"Gentlemen, please follow me," Bishal insists.

Tony turns quick.

"Don't get excited, Baker," he says under his breath. "These crooks will rob you blind, if you're not careful. Let me do the negotiating."

"Tone," I say, setting my hand on his shoulder. "It's not our money we're playing with."

"See, that's always been your problem, daddy's boy. You have no concept of money. If you did, you would have kept the old man's business going even while you write your silly books and travel the world hitting on women."

Anjali turns then, shoots me a sour look.

"Let's not start," I say, as we meet back up with Bishal.

He's standing beside a table that's topped with three drones. Each of them different models but bearing the familiar cross shape. All three sport four, helicopter-like propellers on all four corners, and all of them are armed with cameras in their donut-hole-like centers. About the only difference between them is their size and perhaps their range. Or so it seems.

Bishal stands beside the three drones like he's about to be filmed for a segment on the QVC Shopping Network.

"This first model is the largest but also our most popular model with engineers and real estate professionals," he says, waving his hand over its propellers. "It's a smart little flier because it contains a Wi-Fi module which talks directly with your smartphone. In other words, gentlemen, you see what it sees, while it records video and photos directly to an iOS or Android device in both day and nighttime situations. And best of all, no additional memory cards are needed."

"Range," I ask.

"Twenty-five miles. The maximum for any drone of this sort."

"How much?" Tony says.

"We'll take it," I say.

Tony turns to me. "Way to wheel and deal, kid."

"We're in kind of a rush. And I'm not a kid. I'm forty-something."

"You'll always be a snot-nosed kid to me," Tony says.

"How long does the drone take to charge up, Mr. Bishal?" I say.

The salesman shrugs broad shoulders. "Under

normal circumstances, it could take three hours. That is, you plug it into the wall socket. But I have a device in the back that can power it up in five minutes." He bears brown teeth to go with his Cheshire Cat smile. "Will cost you just a little bit extra, of course."

"Of course," I say. "Just do it, please."

The sweating salesman's face is beaming at the easy sale. He takes the drone and its accompanying hand-held remote control device in hand and slips into the back room. He returns exactly five minutes later with the drone boxed up. Following him back to the front counter, I pay him from what's left of my stack of rupees and we are on our way.

By the time we exit the bazaar, it's going on two in the afternoon.

"We ready to head into the forest?" I pose to Tony, as we come upon his Casale Excavating 4X4.

Everyone looks at one another like "we only have the clothes on our backs." That's because we are only wearing the clothes on our backs. Even the weapons Tony and Rudy used in the firefight at the bar were left behind to burn up along with the bodies of the Thuggee bandits.

"Okay," I say, "I realize we don't have so much as a toothbrush between us, but we can get all that stuff in Dumkibas. Agreed?"

"Time is not on our side," Anjali says, her now tight face a million miles away from the relaxed expression I cuddled with earlier on in the day. "So, let's please do this."

"I could go for a drink," Rudy says.

"We'll pick up some beer later too, Rudy," I say.

He smirks like he only half believes me. Pays to be cynical in a place where you can't just make a pit stop at the corner 7Eleven.

Then I say, "Tony, how long will it take to get to Dumkibas?"

"Depending on traffic getting out of Kathmandu, about three hours. Maybe a little more, or a little less."

"We'll pick up something to eat there as well. Let's get moving."

"Remind me not to hire you as my travel guide, Chase," Tony says.

"This ain't a luxury cruise."

"It ain't no picnic neither," he says, hopping into the Escape, firing up the engine.

WISHING FOR THE ONSET OF DARKNESS.

Because the road to Dumkibas is anything but serene. It's a mountainous journey, the gravel road is narrow and slick from recent rains. As we drive further into the wilderness, we're forced to pass black smoke-spitting buses painted in colorful, almost psychedelic patterns. Passing them wouldn't be so bad if the roads weren't so narrow, the visibility more than a few feet at most. Pulling out into the lane that supports oncoming traffic, all you can do is hold your breath and pray another bus or truck isn't presently coming at you from the opposite direction.

We drive through small towns made up of little more than shanties of scrap wood and tin. The structures are built onto the mountainside (as opposed to into it) with timbers and logs as stilt-like supports. They are connected to the nearest settlement on the opposite side of the deep, dark valley, by means of long rope or cable bridges. The further we drive away from the city and into the heart of Nepal's wilderness, the more strongly we get a sense of how easy it would be to disappear out here. There are no telephone poles, no electrical wires running alongside the roads, only the occasional satellite dish mounted to a tin-roofed shack or a cell tower hastily constructed beside a pile of used tires.

...No wonder Elizabeth disappeared so easily...

It's fully dark when we make it to the perimeter of the Chitwan Forest. Tony drives the mostly flat, dirt road for another twenty or so minutes until we come to the town of Dumkibas, its scattering of dull generator-powered lights illuminating the thick night. Driving slowly into town, we spot a general store constructed of the same tin and scrap wood we've become so accustomed to on the way in. He pulls up out front.

"What's your orders, kid...I mean, Mr. Baker?"

"Been a long time since you asked me that question, Tone."

"Yeah, well, don't get used to it." Making a smirk. "Sentimentality is for pussies."

To our left sits another ramshackle building with a wood sign mounted above the door. It says simply *BAR* in big black letters lit up by a single bare light bulb dangling by an exposed wire from the porch ceiling. There are a couple of dudes hanging out on the porch. They're drinking beer out of bottles. One of them is mid-range height and wiry with a scraggly beard, long hair tied back in a ponytail, and a cowboy hat covering his cranium. He's also wearing a well-worn hunting vest over a black T-shirt that bears the Led Zeppelin logo from the 1970s.

The second guy is shorter, a bit stockier. He's wearing a bush jacket, just like mine. Only difference is, it's somewhat ratty and even from across the road I can make out the dried blood stains that splotch it. The jacket is unbuttoned, exposing the six-gun he's wearing at his hip. His baseball cap is pulled down close to his eyes. It sports the logo of the New York Yankees. I love the Yankees. But I'm not so sure he's the lovable type.

I turn around in the shotgun seat to see that Rudy is dying for a drink. Apparently, happy hour has come and gone. I can take a hint. Chase the perceptive.

"Okay, here's what we're gonna do," I say. "Rudy, you look like you're about to pass out. Go grab a beer and a shot, but make it snappy. It's already dark and I gotta pay somebody extra to take us into those woods under the cover of darkness." Shifting my focus to my employer. "Anjali, you come with us. Take care of the food and water we'll need for upwards of twenty-four hours including something for Elizabeth and your son if and when we finally steal them away." Now Tony. "Tone, you and I will try to gather up some tents, sleeping bags, flashlights, and anything else we need for the jungle."

Tony opens the door, steps out.

Rudy opens the back door. Without a word, he's on his way across the dirt road to the bar, the two dudes on the porch watching him the entire way.

Turns out the general store is the last stop for those traveling the road from civilization into the wild. While Anjali gathers enough freeze-dried food for all of us, Tony and I manage to secure three, two-person tents, sleeping bags, LED flashlights, insect repellent, malaria suppositories, and even a couple of pints of whiskey for Rudy.

The clerk behind the counter, a young Nepalese man with black hair that runs the length of a black and green T-shirt and bears the long-haired likeness of the late Kurt Cobain, also hooks us up with a team of elephants and two out-of-work Sherpas who will take us into the forest within the hour. Anjali finances the entire operation with her American Express.

...Don't leave home without it...

"Elephants," Anjali says, sighing. "My heart breaks for the poor mistreated animals. Why don't we drive? We have a four-wheel-drive vehicle, don't we?"

"First of all," Tony says, "there's no roads where we're going. Second, the jungle is thick and the only practical way to get around, and do so quickly, is by elephant." He issues a satisfied smile. "Just like Hannibal crossing the Pyrenees," he adds.

But Anjali isn't in a laughing mood. She's getting physically closer to her son. The closer we come, the more nervous she seems. It's as if the protective barrier she's managed to construct between her and her emotions over the past many weeks is disintegrating with every step closer to our goal.

Within minutes, we're back outside, the team of elephants being loaded with our gear. We have everything we need to enter the jungle and locate Elizabeth and Rajesh.

Everything but Rudy that is.

That's when the still of the night is shattered by gunshots.

...Heart be still...

"Tony," I say, "stay with Anjali and the equipment."

I run across the street to the bar. Opening the door, I see that Rudy is down on the wood floor, the stocky man with the bush jacket and New York

Yankees baseball cap standing over him, his right booted foot pressed down flat on the Brit's back, his six-shooter in hand.

"What the hell's going on?" I say, as I focus on a bartender who's standing behind the bar, a baseball bat gripped in both his hands.

"That your friend?" says the big, white-aproned barkeep. "Best get him out of here now before he leaves in a pine box."

There's a scattering of disinterested drinkers seated at the bar and three or four empty tables. Apparently, violent contact is as common in this watering hole as stale beer and sweat. The table closest to Rudy has playing cards set out on them. Some of the cards have been strewn onto the floor.

Stocky Baseball Cap turns to face me. As does his partner, the thinner one with the cowboy hat.

"Seems your Union Jack ass-wiping partner doesn't know the rules when it comes to playing a decent game of cards, mate," he says through a thick Australian outback drawl.

...Two big brawls over a simple game of cards in twenty-four hours...my luck—she's not running so good...

I feel the weight of the .45 against my left ribcage. Getting to it quickly might be a challenge what with Stocky Bush Jacket already gripping his piece. Eyeing Tall Cowboy Hat, I see him reaching around his back.

"Easy, Crocodile Dundee," I say. "I'm sure we can figure a way out of this mess without having to shoot our way out."

"I didn't cheat, Chase," Rudy says from down on the floor. "It was a simple game of twenty-one."

"Your pal was dealing," Stocky Bush Jacket says. "Which gave him the right to switch the decks."

"I didn't just switch them, Chase," Rudy insists, his voice muffled and painful. "I just thought a nice fresh deck would be better."

My eyes on Tall Cowboy Hat. "My apologies on behalf of my friend. I'm sure he'll be happy to refund any cash he took off of you."

"Chase, I won that money fair and square," Rudy protests. "Well, mostly anyway."

Tall Cowboy Hat is about to make this a two gun against one gun, gunfight. I need to think quick.

"Jeepers crow, fellas," I add, "What, no one wants a refund?"

"Too late for that, Mate," insists Stocky Bush Jacket. "We'll teach the Brit a lesson in manners, and then teach you some more manners, and then we'll be happy to take our pretty green back with plenty of fucking interest."

Beside me, on my right-hand side, an empty wooden chair. Reaching out, I grab hold of it, toss it at Tall Cowboy Hat. In the split second he's forced to raise up his hands to deflect the chair, I reach into my bush jacket, grab the .45.

"Drop the gun," I say directly to Stocky Bush Jacket while planting a bead on Tall Cowboy Hat. "Do it, or your boyfriend gets a one-way ticket to nirvana. You do believe in nirvana, don't you fellas? Heaven for good people? Hell for bad?"

"You got a way with words, Chase," Rudy says. "Must be the writer in you."

"Rudy. Don't talk. Talk later. Okay?"

"Righto, Chase," he says.

Stocky Baseball Cap isn't budging. He's slowly raising his revolver, his finger on the trigger, his thumb cocking back the hammer.

I thumb back the hammer on the .45.

"You'd better think about what you're doing, pal," I say. "I won't hesitate to air your buddy out."

Even from a distance of fifteen feet, I can see the beads of sweat forming on Tall Cowboy Hat's forehead. When I fire off a round that grazes his shoulder, he drops to his knees, screams.

"Drop your fuckin' gun, Tavis!" the now injured scraggly haired man insists. "The American means business."

"What'll it be, Tavis?" I say. "You gonna listen to your boyfriend, or what?"

Tavis eyes his partner down on his knees.

"Get up, Brucey," he says. "You're embarrassing us."

Brucey brings his fingers to his shoulder, touches his wound.

"I've been shot. I'm fuckin' bleedin'. I'm gonna die."

"Not soon enough you idiot," Tavis says.

"Now," I say. "Brucey can avoid further embarrassment, and certainly further bullets if you take your foot off of my friend and let him up."

"Do it Tavis," Brucey screams. "I mean it, man. It's not worth both of us buying it in this hell hole of a town."

Tavis lowers his gun, slips his foot off of Rudy.

Rudy bounds up onto his feet, faster than I thought the short, overweight, middle-aged bartender capable of doing. He sprints to me, presses himself against me like I'm his long lost dad.

"Walk backward," I say under my breath. "When we come to the door, slip on out."

It's exactly what we do, back-step our way to the door.

"Tavis, Brucey," I say, opening the door, allowing Rudy to slip on out, "It's been a pleasure. Maybe next time we can cook some shrimp on the *barbie*."

"Fuck you very much," Tavis says. "I ain't done with you, Mate."

I slip out the door, slamming it shut behind me.

Five minutes later we've replayed the evening's barroom adventure for the entire crew.

"Whad'd I tell you about getting into fights over silly card games, Rudy?" Tony says, shoving a chunk of fresh chewing tobacco into his cheek. He's clearly upset at his pudgy little friend. "Those two Aussies aren't just a couple of vacationers. They're poachers who'll shoot you dead, cut up your little puff ball body, and feed ya to the tigers in the forest."

Rudy cocks his head over his shoulder like a little boy caught with his hand in a cookie jar full of booze.

"Well, it's all about how you play the game," he says, smiling slyly. "And you know what I always say: Rudy can't fail." He sings "Rudy can't fail" like Joe Strummer from The Clash.

We gather around the back of the general store where the elephants are waiting. Four elephants to act as rides and two more for storage. The two small, leather-skinned Sherpas will walk ahead of us.

"Tony," I say, "what about the Ford? The getaway vehicle? I think I put those Aussies in their place for now, but I don't trust them not to do some damage to our only means of transport out of this place."

"Under a tarp in a patch of woods," he says, nodding toward a wooded area not far away from the store's backside. "Nobody will bother her there." Then, "Also, our general store sells more than camping equipment. He raises the tail on his denim work shirt to reveal an automatic, the barrel of which is stuffed inside his pant waist.

"Nine millimeter?" I say.

"Of course," he says. "I need to rely on stopping power."

"Let's hope you don't have to."

Now, with everyone mounted and the Sherpas out ahead of us with Maglites poking bright holes in the thick darkness, I give the order to proceed.

"Let's find Elizabeth," I say.

"Alive," Anjali says. "Just like Rajesh."

"Yes," I say, my heart suddenly sinking into my stomach, "let's hope we haven't made this trip for nothing."

19

WE TRUDGE THROUGH THE THICK FOREST FOR MORE than an hour, only the occasional mosquito stealing its share of blood from my veins breaking up the monotony but, at the same time, adding to the tension. The jungle is a different world at night. It's when the place comes alive. Beneath a canopy of trees, every animal, insect, and bird comes out of its hiding place in search of food and love.

At night, the noise in the jungle can be deafening, but it can also be a spooky place with vampire bats sweeping down so close to your head you feel as if they're touching you with their fur-covered skin. Sticky cobwebs as thick as shoelaces smack you in the face as the elephants transport you between a narrow opening created by two iron trees.

I take the lead while Anjali rides directly behind

me. Behind her is Rudy, who's drinking whiskey from one of the pint bottles and whistling a tune the entire time like he's not got a care in the world. Riding on our tail is Tony. Behind him, the two supply elephants. When I feel we've gone far enough into the jungle, I give the order to stop and set up camp.

"Tony," I say, as the elephant bends down on its front knees and I slide down off its back, "grab up the drone."

It's time we make our first attempt at locating the exact location of our diamond mine.

The Sherpas set up the tents and gather firewood while Tony and I power up the drone. Anjali is in charge of monitoring her smartphone with the real-time visuals of whatever the drone picks up with its multiple cameras. If my hunch serves me correctly, the bastards who took Elizabeth hostage will be working around the clock to mine the diamond deposit for its infinite riches. And if that's indeed true, the spot in which they're working should be lit up like a Christmas tree.

Unpacking the drone, we need a place in the forest where we're not surrounded by trees. Lucky for us, the jungle territory inside and outside the boundaries of the Chitwan National Forest contains as many open plains of tall grass as it does deep cover. Following the light of the moon, we walk towards an opening that's no more than one hundred paces from our camp. From this point on, it's just a matter of powering up the droid and synching the infrared night-vision camera with Anjali's iPhone. When the camera sync is complete, I set the drone onto the grassy floor while Tony powers it up via the remote control.

"You ever use these before, Tony?"

"You're not an excavator unless you have one of these in your arsenal these days," he says. "There's no more accurate way to lay out a site, believe me. Your father would have loved these little babies. Plus they're fun to fly. It's a goddamned toy."

"Tony, you have changed, my friend. Smartphones, computers, unmanned drones. What's next, Google Glasses?"

"I got me a pair of them too. Probably burned up in the fire you started. I'll add them to my bill."

He thumbs some switches on the remote and suddenly, the drone propellers come to life with a low-key, buzzsaw sound. A moment after that, we have lift off. While the drone quickly gains altitude, I peer over Anjali's shoulder and focus in on the smartphone screen. I see the jungle floor we occupy, our bodies illuminated in a bright orange glow. I even wave at myself down here on the ground.

"What's our range?" I ask Tony.

"We can operate this baby safely within a radius of twenty miles. Elizabeth and the assholes who took her are any further out than that, we're screwed anyway."

"How will you know which direction to go?" Anjali asks.

"I start by making small circles and then I'll make like a corkscrew and increase the radius a little bit more and a little bit more with each revolution until I find them."

"A plan as good as any," I say.

We stand in silence while the drone performs its reconnaissance mission, scouring the forest for any sign of artificial light besides our own. The machine makes six or seven full circular sweeps before Anjali's screen begins to broadcast something other than pitch darkness. A dim light begins to bleed into the small rectangular screen. Barely noticeable at first, but getting brighter all the time, as the silhouette of the leafy treetops begin to take shape.

"Try and tighten the circle to the northeast, Tone. We've got something."

Anjali inverts her smartphone, reveals the picture to Tony.

"Okay," he says, "I'm just gonna make a few figure eights in a northeasterly direction."

Within a few seconds, the project comes into view. An area about the size of an acre, lit up with mobile lamps. The infrared light is picking up bodies moving back and forth from what looks to be an opening in the ground, like a man-made tunnel. The opening appears to be hidden by a tin-roofed shack. It's exactly how I relay it to Anjali and Tony.

"Can we zoom in at all, Tone?"

He does it. The camera zooms in close enough so that I can see the vague faces of men dressed in black robes, boots, and matching turbans, automatic weapons slung over their shoulders. They're guarding another group of men and women who are scantily dressed and wheeling wheel barrels out of the tunnel opening, depositing their contents onto conveyor crusher belts that feed flat vibrating screens which I know from experience serve as sieves or sifters.

"Holy crap," I say, "they've employed slave labor to do the digging."

"Funny way to put," Anjali says. "Employed."

"What about Elizabeth?" Tony says. "Do you see her?"

Anjali and I stare down at the phone, at the pathetic people coming and going from the cave with their wheel barrels. But there's something else going on too. As the drone camera shifts further east, the ground seems to open up wide as if it weren't ground at all, but a giant mouth. There's a bright light emanating from the opening. Light isn't even the right word for it. More like an earthly sun glowing or radiating from out of the ground.

"Need more detail!" I bark at Tony.

"Let me adjust the contrast on the camera," he says.

The brightness of the illumination is shielded somewhat to reveal a hard surface that glows. The surface must be at least one hundred feet wide by the same distance long. Surrounding the glowing surface on all sides are worshipers. It's hard to tell, but I'm guessing they're all men, all of them dressed in black, down on their knees as though praying in reverence before the opening.

It hits me then.

"The diamond deposit," I say. "That can be the only explanation."

"But I thought the map engraved on the back of the Kali Statue was supposed to lead us to the diamond deposit," Anjali says. "I'm not following."

The camera continues to move, continues to focus in on the deposit. Soon, I begin to make out something situated in the center of the glowing deposit. It's a statue.

"More focus, Tone," I insist. "More zoom. Hold the drone's position right there."

"Okay," he answers. "She's hovering. But it's only a matter of time before one of those religious fanatics spots it."

As the picture on the smartphone zooms in, I begin to make out the statute. It's about the size of a large human being. It's the eight-armed golden Kali. She's seated in lotus position, a portion of her lower body embedded into the deposit itself as if it the statue were miraculously born from out of the mammoth diamond.

"The Golden Kali Statue wasn't the source of a map at all," I say. "It was a marker. Elizabeth finally found it. And at the same time, revealed it to Kashmiri."

"At gun point no doubt," Tony points out.

There's something else going on too. A commotion coming from the crowd as they split in two. Two big men are dragging someone by her arms towards the diamond deposit. The woman has long hair, and she's wearing a black shawl.

"Holy Christ that's Elizabeth," I say, my heart sinking into my stomach as if it were made of rock.

She's clearly struggling. Clearly not wanting anything to do with what's happening. The two big men proceed to lead her out onto the glowing diamond deposit before chaining each of her arms to what appear to be two concrete pillars set before the Kali statue. My heart pounds. I want to scream at her to get out. To run. But I'm powerless.

"My God, Chase, what are they doing to her?" Anjali says.

"I don't know for sure," I say swallowing something bitter and dry. "I've only seen it in old documentary movies, but I'm beginning to think this is the start of a Thuggee ceremony. And if that's the case, she's in deep trouble."

As the two men leave her, a kind of billowing smoke rises from the surface of the diamond deposit as if it's heating up. Two more figures enter the scene. One man is tall and black-bearded. He's also wearing a black robe and turban, wrapped around his waist is a blood-red sash. He's also holding a staff.

"Kashmiri," I whisper. Then, "Tony, how far away

are we from the diamond deposit? I need to get to Elizabeth. Get to them now."

"You'll never make it, Chase. It's twelve or thirteen miles out through thick jungle, minimum."

I feel almost faint I'm so panicked by the sight of the ceremony. There's not a damn thing I can do other than stand there and watch.

"Do you see Rajesh?" Anjali begs, panic in her voice.

Another object appears on the screen. It's a mobile platform being pulled by two Thuggees. Chained to the platform is a little boy with six arms. The boy is outfitted in a gold turban, gold tunic and pants, his feet bare. Because of the spotlights and the glow from the diamond deposit, the drone camera is able to pick up the sparkling light that's shining off the many diamonds he wears on all thirty of his fingers.

"Rajesh," Anjali screams, slapping her hand against her mouth.

I wrap my arm around her.

"It's okay," I say. "He's alive and that's what counts."

As soon as Kashmiri comes to the edge of the diamond deposit, he spreads his arms and stares up at the dark night sky. Raising his black staff, it appears that he's begun to chant something. Chant something to the Gods maybe. Because we're not always picking up audio, there's no way to make out exactly what he's saying. But just watching his intensity makes my heart pound. Behind him, it appears the worshippers begin chanting along with him. They're now down on all fours, banging their foreheads on the hard ground, as though inflicting pain on their own bodies is a way of summoning something evil up from the very depths of the earth.

My heart beats harder. Mouth goes dry. Throughout my adventures, I've witnessed physical proof of a divine God and even proof of alien beings. But never before have I come face to face with Satan. The smoke coming from the deposit grows more and more intense while the surface takes on a red/orange glow. Elizabeth struggles against the chains that bind her. She's in great pain. I can feel her pain even from where I'm standing. Meanwhile, the boy seems to be trembling, shaking, as he enters into a convulsive state.

"What are they going to do to her, Chase?" Anjali cries out. Then, "What's happening to Rajesh?"

I turn to her. "Don't look at it."

Something extraordinary happens then. The earth seems to shake, and Kashmiri begins to levitate. His body lifts up and he is carried by a power not of this world over the surface of the smoking, glowing diamond deposit. The closer the bearded man comes to Elizabeth, the more she struggles against the chains.

When finally he is upon her, he reaches inside his robes with his free hand, produces a dagger shaped like a crescent moon. He holds the dagger up to the heavens as if for inspection. The earth shakes once more and a bolt of lightning flashes from the sky to the tip of the blade. For a brief moment the drone trembles and shakes.

"Easy baby," Tony says, his hands maneuvering the remote controls. "I can't hold the drone for much longer, Chase. Not if we wanna get her back in one piece."

Elizabeth…

I want to respond to Tony. But my throat has closed up on itself, my pulse speeding so rapidly I feel like I might pass out. But I can't pass out. Won't pass out. Part of me wants to run. To save Elizabeth and the boy. But that's crazy. They're a dozen miles away inside a remote portion of jungle. It would take me ten or more hours to get to her. Like I said, no choice but to stand there helplessly, hopelessly...impotently.

Elizabeth...

The lightning disappears as the blade of the dagger takes on the same glow as the diamond deposit. Then, as kneeling worshippers raise up their torsos and their hands, Kashmiri thrusts the blade into Elizabeth's chest.

"No!" Anjali screams.

"Look away!" I insist. "Do not look at the screen anymore. You hear me?"

"Do it, Anjali," Tony insists. "Listen to Chase. Look away now."

Kashmiri twists the knife in a circular motion until he has cut a perfect circle in her chest. Returning the knife to its scabbard, he reaches inside with the now free hand, pulls out her heart.

Elizabeth...Do you believe in love at first sight?

The drone's audio manages to pick up a scream.

But the scream is not coming from Elizabeth. It's the kind of scream that can only come from a little boy in distress. In pain.

Elizabeth, I love you...I...love...you...

The earth beneath me feels as if it has dropped away. My head spins while an orchestra of screams and shrieks fills my brain. Kashmiri turns, holds the heart up for his worshipers who now raise up their bodies and their arms, praising the presence of Elizabeth's still beating heart. Looking at her face, I can tell she's not quite dead, but instead moving her mouth as if trying to shout, but unable to. The glow from the diamond deposit increases to an almost blood red, as the heart goes still in Kashmiri's hand and Elizabeth's mouth stops moving, her soul departing her body. At the same time, the vaporous smoke rising from the deposit begins to take the shape of a giant skull, its eyes glowing yellow/orange, a pair of sharp horns protruding from the top of its cranium.

Anjali, her eyes closed, is reciting the Our Father prayer aloud.

"Kali is summoned," I mumble, the words barely making it out of my mouth.

Kashmiri raises the heart, then brings it to his mouth, taking a large bite out of it. Once more raising his staff up to the heavens, he is then transported across the surface of the diamond deposit as it erupts into bright red flame. As a final sacrifice to Kali, he tosses what's left of Elizabeth's heart into the fire as the rest of her body is incinerated.

"They've done it," I say, tears of rage and sadness filling my eyes. "Resurrected the Thuggee god. They've reincarnated Kali."

Maybe a half minute passes before the flames disappear and, along with them, any sign of Elizabeth Flynn's body. Kashmiri takes his place before Rajesh, bows his head in reverence while the boy's body begins convulsing, as though acting as the catalyst for summoning Kali has sucked the life right out of him. The ceremony over, the worshippers stand, shoulder their AK47s and begin to shoot indiscriminate rounds into the air. It's as if they are ready to go to war with the world, kill anyone who doesn't prescribe to their black magic. Their evil.

That's when I notice a couple of the black-robed guards who are taking up the rear of the procession. They appear to be communicating. When one of them looks up at the night sky, points directly at the camera, I know we've been made.

"Bring her in, Tony," I say, wiping my eyes with the backs of my hand. "We've been spotted."

Just then, both guards take aim with their weapons, plant their separate beads. We see the muzzle flashes and just like that, the image on Anjali's smartphone goes dead.

"So much for one slightly used drone," Tony says, tossing the remote control into the bush.

"Anjali, do we still have the GPS coordinates?"

She finishes the prayer, peers up at the night sky, makes another sign of the cross over her chest. Then, breathing in deeply, she runs her hands through her hair which has become thick with perspiration.

"Got them," she assures, having gathered her composure. Her voice, however, still trembling from the Thuggee ceremony. "Saved."

"Let's get back to camp and consult a map," I say, my voice cracking. Grabbing my walkie-talkie from my pocket, I radio Rudy. "Rudy, come in. Rudy. You there?" Releasing my thumb, I wait and listen. But all I get is static. "Rudy man, come on, you there?" Nothing. Then, to Tony and Anjali, "Rudy's probably into his second pint by now. Let's just go."

But first, Tony reaches out, grabs my arm.

"Chase," he says, his eyes wide, not blinking. "You okay?"

I nod. "I'm not sure what I feel."

"She didn't suffer. You hear me? She didn't suffer."

"The fucker cut her heart out, Tone. He cut her heart out. Don't tell me she didn't suffer."

He releases my arm.

"Let's just go," he says.

We hump the three hundred feet through the

darkness to the camp. Although the distance is short, it takes a while to break through the tall grass with the machetes in the night. But it's then, for the first time since Dr. Singh approached me in Piazza Santa Maria Novella in Florence, that this thing is beginning to make sense. What was once a three-part mystery has now merged into one single, well-connected plot of insidiousness.

This is no longer simply about rescuing a little boy born with a congenital deformity that a handful of religious zealots interpreted as a God-like attribute. It's no longer the search for a legendary diamond deposit that might provide an entire army with the cash it needs to wage a war of evil and terrorism. It's no longer about confirming the truth about Elizabeth.

This is about Satan himself being summoned from the depths of Hell by a known terrorist turned Thuggee. An animal capable of ripping the heart out of an innocent woman's chest while it's still beating.

This is no longer just a job. It's now become personal.

What does personal mean, exactly?

It means that no matter what happens with the God Boy, I will find Kashmiri, and I will find a way to eradicate him from the earth...as slowly and painfully as possible.

The light of the fire in our camp is a welcome sight.

But what's far from welcome is the first thing I see when breaking through the brush.

I see Rudy, his hands tied behind his back, a noose wrapped around his neck.

THEY MUST HAVE FOLLOWED US HERE THE ENTIRE WAY.
But it wasn't until we left camp to put up the drone,
that they made their move.

Aussie Tavis and Aussie Bruce...The angry
gamblers...The poachers.

They're positioned four-square on either side of
Rudy, who is standing...no, scratch that...who is
precariously *balancing* himself on one of the small
collapsible tables the Sherpas packed for the trek, the
rope wrapped around his neck tied off to a thick
branch belonging to a nearby iron tree. Situated not
far behind him, the Sherpas themselves, tied together
at the wrists, seated on the ground, facing away from
one another, their mouths covered with strips of duct
tape, as if there's anyone to hear their screams out
here in this heavily forested nowhere.

A fire is burning in a shallow pit in the center of camp and the tents have been set up a dozen or so feet away from it. The elephants are not visible since they're hidden by the brush, but I can hear them rustling uncomfortably about, yanking on the thick ropes and chains that secure them to the tree trunks.

The New York Yankees baseball cap-wearing Tavis is once more holding his revolver while the cowboy-hatted Bruce has a scope-mounted 30.06 bolt-action Springfield gripped in both his hands, port arms position. Apparently, the bullet that grazed his shoulder just a few hours ago isn't bothering him all that much. But then, maybe he's too drunk to notice. Or too drugged up. Or just too much of an asshole.

Rudy is trembling, the table beneath him looking like it's about to tip or even crumble under his weight, simple physics the only thing keeping him from entering into the kingdom of heaven before his allotted time.

"Rudy," I say. "Be still. I'm gonna get you out of this."

Tony reaches for his gun, takes a threatening step forward. But Tavis aims quick, fires off a round that hits the dirt only a few inches from the excavator's feet. Anjali screams, presses herself up against me.

"Down on your knees, digger man," Tavis says. "Hands over your head. Do it now."

Tony drops to his knees, locks his fingers together at the knuckles, rests them on his cranial cap.

"They know you, Tone?" I say out the corner of my mouth.

"Nepal is a small town, believe you me," he says. "Kathmandu is even smaller. These two kangaroos have gotten themselves kicked out of every bar in the city, including mine. I almost said something about it earlier, but I never imagined this happening."

"Shut your mouth, digger," Tavis says. But then, his face lights up like he just remembered it's his birthday.

"What have we here?" he says, his wet-eyed smile reminiscent of a bad guy in a Clint Eastwood spaghetti western...*The Good, the Bad, and the Totally Fucked*. "A lady, all the way out here in the middle of nowhere. And I thought that hanging your pal, Rudy, was going to be for male eyes only."

I can feel Anjali's body trembling against me.

"What do you want, Tavis?" I say. "I thought we settled this in town."

He smiles. "The only thing we settled was the fate of your mate, Rudy, here...and all the rest of you. And you thought I was being reasonable."

"They're gonna kill us, Chase," Tony whispers over his shoulder. "No one will find our bodies out here."

Tavis starts walking towards me, the black barrel of his revolver staring me down like the Grim Reaper while my .45 sits idle inside my shoulder holster. When he's within a couple of feet, he reaches out, snatches Anjali by the arm, pulls her away from me. Instinct kicks in, and I reach out for her, but he cold cocks me across the side of my head with his piece. I go down on my side, my head spinning, the pain coming and going with every rapid beat of my pulse. I feel a hand rummaging around inside my jacket and my .45 being snatched out.

"You bastard," Tony says. "You don't know who you're dealing with, poacher boy."

From the ground, I see Tavis pulling Anjali by her hair. He's trying to kiss her neck while she pushes him away. The ear to ear smile he wears proves how much he's enjoying himself.

"Let me show you what you're dealing with," he says. Then, shooting his partner a look. "Do it, Brucey."

Shouldering his rifle, Bruce takes aim at the rickety table, fires.

The stool beneath Rudy disintegrates.

The bartender drops, the noose catching his neck as the rope goes taught. But it hasn't killed him instantly, and he begins to kick and flail while the noose slowly chokes him to death.

The entire world seems to be spinning out of control, the pain in my head is suddenly accompanied by nausea in my stomach. Anjali is screaming, trying to claw her way out of Tavis's grip while Rudy is only moments away from asphyxiating to death. It's then that I hear another kind of choking coming from Tony. Peering at him from where I'm kneeling on the jungle floor, I seem him grasping at his throat, foamy spittle spewing forth from his mouth.

"Snake bite," he barks, his voice panicked and constricted like no air is passing through his throat into his lungs. "Snake...bite!"

Tavis's eyes go wide. He releases Anjali.

"Snake?" he says, jumping in place, his eyes peeled to the jungle floor. "What snake? Where?"

"Ha ha ha," Bruce says, his 30.06 still gripped in both hands. "Tavis don't like snakes."

Inhaling deeply, I stare into Tony's pain-filled face. He issues me the slightest of smiles and a wink of his eye. And then, he lunges for Tavis.

Tony catches the poacher around the ankles, takes him down like a defensive end sacking a quarterback. Tavis falls hard, his revolver dropping out of his hand. He reaches for it, so desperate to regain control of the weapon he is clawing at the ground. Tony is able to reach it first, turning the revolver on its owner. Tavis raises himself up onto his knees, lifts up his hands in surrender, works up a smile.

"Don't....shoot," he says with a swallow, his Adam's apple bobbing up and down in his throat. Then, smiling. "We can work this out, mate."

Raising his 30.06, Brucey shoulders the weapon. Tony catches the cowboy-hatted poacher out the corner of his eye, plants a bead, fires. Brucey drops on the spot. Dead. Then, pointing the barrel at the rope from which Rudy dangles, he fires again. The ropes snaps in two and the Brit falls to the jungle floor, his hands wrap around the noose as he manages to pull it loose. It's a magnificent shot.

Tony turns the gun once more on Tavis.

"Wail you son of a whore," he says.

"What?" Tavis says, his face ashen, dripping sweat.

"Cry like a gut-shot elephant," he insists while thumbing back the hammer.

"Why?"

"Because I want you to know how an elephant feels just before you shoot it in the gut before cutting off its tusks and leaving it there to die and rot."

Tony triggers a round that takes half the poachers left ear clean off in an explosion of flesh and dark blood.

Tavis screams, blood running down the left side of his face and neck.

"Wail!" Tony insists, thumbing back the trigger once more.

The now pale-faced Tavis inhales a deep breath, begins making a sound not like an elephant, but more like a wounded dog. High pitched, desperate, and ugly. Tony shifts the revolver barrel just a couple of inches to the left, fires again, taking most of the poacher's right ear off.

Tavis screams again, the right side of his face now covered in blood and little bits of jagged, dangling flesh.

"Please....stop!!!"

He's screaming so loudly it's a wonder the Thuggees can't hear it all those miles away. But then, not even noise from the shots we've fired can penetrate this thick jungle.

"I'll gladly stop," Tony says. "But not until every elephant in this forest gets their money's worth."

Lowering the revolver, he takes aim at Tavis's left leg, fires. The poacher's knee explodes. He drops onto his side, his wailing now having de-evolved into outright sobbing.

"Please," the poacher pleads, "for the love of God."

"This one's for God," Tony says. "For the love of his most magnificent of creations...the mighty elephants."

Tony plants a bead, blows Tavis's other knee away.

Then, shoving the pistol barrel into his pant waist, "Give me a hand will you, Chase?"

He makes his way over to Tavis, grabs hold of his left forearm. Following Tony's lead, I grab onto the right forearm and together we begin to drag the poacher back into the thick forest. Then, opening the cylinder on the pistol, Tony makes a check on how many fresh rounds the poacher's got left.

"Looks like I was counting correctly," he says as he hands the pistol back to Tavis, who's lying there on his back, bleeding out, writhing in pain. At the same time, Tony retrieves my .45, hands it back to me.

"You're just...gonna...leave me...here?" Tavis poses.

"That's exactly what we're gonna do, Mate," Tony says. "Just like you leave them gut-shot elephants to die a slow, agonizing death just so you can make a few bucks on the ivory black market."

Then, his angry eyes focused on me. "Come on."

We head back in the direction of the camp.

We don't cover more than thirty feet of ground before we hear the shot that tells us Tavis, the Poacher, is fast on a one-way trip to hell.

"CHRIST, TONE," I SAY, **"WHERE'D YOU LEARN TO** shoot like that?"

I also want to ask him how he went from being a simple tough-guy-earth-mover to Dirty Harry in a just half a decade. But one thing at a time.

"You don't know everything about me, Son," he says, popping another bit of tobacco in his mouth. "I used to shoot with your dad now and again. I just got better at it while living out here. You know the right people, you can buy a gun on the street here. Don't need a license." He spits tobacco juice on the jungle floor, smiles proudly. "And I know the right people."

When we get to the camp, Rudy is stealing small sips of whiskey while applying an antibiotic ointment to the red and swollen, rope-shaped irritation banded around his neck.

"A mere few hours ago, I was a simple barkeep at an establishment I'd just sold off for pennies in the heart of Kathmandu," he says, his gruff voice sounding like his tonsils were just removed. "Since then, the bar's been burned down, I've been held at gunpoint for cheating at cards, and I've been hanged by the neck. What's next, the earth opening beneath my feet to reveal the devil?"

I wonder if Rudy realizes just how accurate his prediction might turn out.

Anjali is seated by the fire. She's staring into it, her eyes glowing and distant. Not a few feet away from her lies the bled out body of Aussie Bruce.

"Rudy and Tony," I say, "untie the Sherpas and have them bury the bodies."

Tony pulls out his knife, cuts the Sherpas loose. Then, having instructed them on what do to about the poachers, they begin hauling Bruce into the same section of forest where his partner breathed his last. Tony and Rudy accompany the paid help, but before disappearing into the dark woods, the former Baker Excavating employee turns to me.

"These Sherpas hate the poachers as much as I do. They'd rather the bodies are left behind for the vultures."

"Far be it from me to break with the will of the masses," I say.

The men disappear into the bush with Bruce. Making my way to Anjali, I take a knee beside her.

"You okay?"

She nods as a single tear falls from her eye, runs down her smooth cheek.

"I was convinced I was about to be killed," she says. Then, wiping the tear from her eye with the back of her hand. "Allow me to correct myself, Chase. I was convinced I was about to be raped, tortured, then killed. In that precise order." She sniffles, wipes her eyes. "But I'm not crying for me. I'm crying for Rajesh, his screams, the sweet, gentle soul that's being robbed from his body. I'm also crying for Elizabeth...for what Kashmiri did to her." She looks up at me. "But yes, I was also afraid for my own life and I'm not certain I deserve to be afraid for me."

Exhaling. "Fear. Kind of goes with the job."

She shoots me a look like I've just tried to cop an unwelcome feel.

"Goes with the job?" she says. "But you seem to *like* the job."

I cock my head over my shoulder. "I'm good at it. That's why people like your ex, Dr. Singh, hire me."

She refocuses her gaze into the fire. "I suppose you're right. Singh wouldn't trust you with finding Rajesh if he weren't convinced you were the right man for the job."

Reaching out my hand, I gently set it on her shoulder.

"And true to my word," I say, "I've found him."

Her eyes light up. What had been tears of sadness are now replaced with at least a small measure of joy, or relief anyway. Relief that can only come from someone who's experienced the loss of a loved one, only to find out he or she is alive.

She looks me in the eye.

"You have to believe me, Chase. I only want one thing. And that's to see my boy returned to me. He doesn't have long to live. His unusual physical condition assures that. There's only so much time left for him to love me and me to love him."

"If Kashmiri has his way, your God Boy will be leading a great army that will be invincible. Listen carefully..."

She places her hand on my arm. "You need to know how sorry I am about the loss of Elizabeth."

"Thanks. But she wasn't mine anyway. She made that perfectly clear a long time ago."

"But the way Singh promised her to you...promised her alive. Your heart must be broken for a second time, regardless of what happened between you and me back at the hotel."

I try to feel my heart. Sure it's pumping the blood I need to survive, to live and breathe, but I can't feel it. Or maybe it's more accurate to say, I don't *want* to feel it. Maybe it's been broken too many times before, and now it sits there inside my ribcage cobbled back together with scar tissue, bruises, and regrets. My heart aches not only for the woman I've loved and lost but also for a daughter who will experience most of her fourth-grade year in New York City without my being around for it.

My heart tells me I should stick around more and be there for her whenever she needs me. But my body needs to get up and go, like a man who just can't sit still. My ex-wife was convinced my problem was deeply psychological. Pathological even. Maybe she was right. Maybe I have a sickness and don't even know it. Don't want to know it.

I stare into Anjali's dark eyes and I feel for her because she is so worried about her boy. But, then I'm reminded that she and Singh split up over the boy and that somehow Kashmiri abducted him even if she hasn't yet revealed to me the precise manner in which the abduction came to be. But then, maybe she doesn't want me to know. Maybe the circumstances of the abduction are something she and Singh would rather forget since it happened on their watch.

Tony and Rudy break through the woods, the

Sherpas a few steps behind them. Rudy's neck still looks sore, but at least it's not snapped in half. Tony has a look in his eyes I recall all too well from my days as a soldier in Desert Storm. It's what we old grunts call "the million-mile" stare. I know he's sensing not only imminent danger but also pure evil to go along with it. The worst is yet to come.

"We should all get some sleep," I say. "We'll start out at first light for Kashmiri's encampment and diamond mine."

Rudy takes a drink from his bottle, drags the back of his hand across his mouth.

"Do we get to eat anything?" he says. "I'm starving. Hanging by the neck takes a lot out of you."

Anjali's eyes go wide. "How the hell can you talk about food at a time like this? Rajesh is being held captive by a devil and we're just sitting here."

I turn to her. "We're going to get him out of there. I promise you that, Anjali." Then to Tony. "It's important that everyone tries to eat. Our energy reserves will begin to run low in this jungle heat."

"You know me, Chase," he says. "I'm always up for food." But I know he's lying.

Approaching the Sherpas, I instruct them to cook up something simple and quick using the freeze-dried food supplies. In the meantime, Tony and I come up with a plan for extracting Rajesh from that diamond mine. It's the least I can do to divert my thoughts from the now dead Elizabeth. A woman I loved with all my heart, but not for long.

22

THE SHERPAS COOK US A SIMPLE LENTIL CURRY WHICH we eat with small slabs of naan, their traditional flatbread. Rather, I *attempt* to eat, but visions of Elizabeth being murdered atop the diamond deposit is too much to take for my heart and stomach. When the plates are cleared, Rudy and Anjali retire to their tents. I need to keep myself busy or I'll think too much. Remember too much. Which means Tony and I look over a topo map of the jungle and work on our plan for stealing the kid away from Kashmiri.

With the topo map laid out before us, I match up the GPS coordinates retrieved from the drone to the precise area on the map where both the diamond mine and the Thuggee encampment and tunnel are located. Turns out, we're talking an area the size of several football fields, which is how I describe it to Tony.

"But we need to concentrate only on one place," he says. "The tunnel."

"Who knows how long, how wide, how deep that tunnel is. If it were built into the side of a hill or a mountain, we might be able to make reasonable sense of it. But underground like that, who knows. It could zigzag for miles like an ant farm. No telling what kind of surprises wait for us inside, we even manage to get inside. What kind of security?"

"My guess is that it's several layers deep, with stairs and elevators. A real working mine, which means..." He looks up at me like he's just experienced his Eureka moment.

"Which means what, Tone?"

"You and I have worked on enough underground tunnel and cave projects through the years to know that every single one of them, no matter how big or how small, no matter how sophisticated or simplistic, have one very important thing in common."

He slaps his chest as if to give me a clue.

"Air," I say. "They all need air shafts to pump oxygen in and CO_2 out."

"Canary in a coal mine," he says. "Since we don't have shit in the way of weaponry, going Stallone and blasting our way in and out won't cut it."

"We'll drown them in their own air."

"Now you're cooking with Wesson, Baker. And when the time comes for that kid to show his face, we snatch him up and make a run for it."

"Won't be that easy. Could be he'll be attached at the hip to Kashmiri, and if that's the case, we'll need aforementioned weapons, be they ever so humble."

"Well, he's just a man and those black-robed Thuggee soldiers surrounding him are just flesh and blood no matter how much they try and pull off their

Darth Vader thing. They put on their socks just like us in the morning. Trust me, bullets and knives will pierce their skin." He smiles. "But here's where we harbor a distinct advantage. We can commandeer Bruce's scoped 30.06. As the nasties make their exit from the tunnel, we can pick them off one by one. It'll be fun. Like a video game."

"Not enough rounds for that."

"But we give the impression we have enough rounds. You see, we form a semi-circle around their front perimeter, Anjali shooting from one spot, myself from another, and you from another. When the Thuggees run for cover, that's our signal to move in and make the extraction."

Standing, sighing.

"That's the plan," I say, my tone less than confident.

"Only one we got. And it's as good as any. Or maybe you as the boss man can do better?"

"Why do I feel like we've suddenly been transported back in time and we're working for my old man on some excavation project in some remote part of the world?"

"Well, you got remote part of the world right anyway."

"I appreciate the input, Tone, and your plans aren't all that bad. I'm just not sure how practical they are."

"What's that mean, Chase?"

"It means, whenever I've had to do an extraction, be it with civilian boots or army issue boots on, it usually went down one way and one way only: I thumbed off the safety on my hand cannon, ran in after my target, pressed a little C-4 against the cell door, set it off, grabbed the *extractee* by the collar, dragged him back out of the place. We'd already be gone by the time anyone figured out what just happened."

"Stealth and surprise," Tony nods. "You're talkin' stealth and surprise like an Apache Indian."

"Precisely."

We pause for a beat while a knot forms in my stomach and I contemplate all the many ways I might have extracted Elizabeth from that diamond mine if only I'd had the chance. Then, "You take first watch?"

Tony's eyes shift from me to Anjali's tent back to me again. He smiles.

"It's not like that," I say.

He shoots me a wink while a single droplet of sweat slowly falls down his unshaven cheek.

"Sure it's not," he says. Then, his grin turns into a frown. "Elizabeth. You thought she would…"

"Yes," I say before he can get the words out. "I thought she might…live."

"Just remember," he says, "you're alive. And the life we lead by chasing after fortune and fame, well…you never know. Anything can happen. Bad or good."

Now it's my turn to smile. But I can't honestly say it has anything to do with happiness.

"You never know," I say. "Love the one you're with, right?"

"I grew up in the sixties. That's my motto."

He grabs his .9mm by the grip, pulls back the slide, cocks a round into the chamber.

"I'll be sitting in a tree case you need anything, Baker."

"What could I possibly need from you," I say, as he disappears into the darkness.

Moments later, I lie on my back inside my tent, my shirt and T-shirt removed in the hot, humid heat, but my pants and boots still on, just in case I need to move quickly. The only thing you can truly expect in the jungle is the unexpected. Or so I warn myself over and over again.

"Life is a jungle," I whisper. "I like the jungle...need the jungle. Elizabeth needed the jungle too. Needed to be searching. And when she found what she wanted, she died for it."

It's as if she knew I was watching. That somehow fate had intervened one final time and waited for my arrival to the jungle, just so I could witness her final, horrible moments chained to those pilasters above the open diamond mine, only inches away from the Golden Kali Statue she desired for so long.

I close my eyes, wait for the onset of sleep. But I know my efforts will be futile. I listen to the insects buzzing all around me. The howls of the spider monkeys. Snakes slither in the grass outside my tent—paralysis and death in their venomous bite. Black spiders crawl up and down the tent poles, spinning their webs. Bats swoop down from overhead while tigers eye their prey in the deep heart of darkness.

The entire lethal world feels alive. But I feel dead inside.

Maybe I could have saved Elizabeth if I hadn't wasted so much time getting to the jungle from Kathmandu. But then, I hadn't wasted any time. Her fate was sealed before those elephants carried us into the forest. Hell, her fate was sealed before Singh hired me. It was sealed the moment I left her standing there on the train platform five years ago in Varanasi.

Then, a sound, coming from outside the tent. Like an animal trying to get in.

I reach for my automatic, plant a bead on whatever it is that's about to enter my portable domicile. When the tent flap flips up and I see the figure of a woman in the half light, my brain thinks, *Elizabeth*. But that's impossible. It is instead, Anjali. Her hair has been let down and it drapes her narrow shoulders like a smooth black veil. She's wearing a white tank top and a pair of black panties. Her feet are bare.

Without a word, she crawls over to me, onto me.

Then, "You should have worn your boots," I say. "Snakes thrive out there."

"I'm sorry," she whispers. "I know you suffered a great loss today. I haven't been very good about it. Forgive me. But now I just want you to hold me and if you allow it, I'd like to hold you in return."

I squeeze her tightly and inhale her rose petal scent. I feel her hair against my face and I feel my heart beating. After a time, my eyes close and the deadly world around me goes quiet.

I sleep the restless sleep of a broken-hearted man, until...

...my body slips out from under Anjali's. Slips out of the tent as though lifted by invisible gods so that I feel myself effortlessly rising into the night sky. When I'm above the treeline, my body stops its ascent and hovers over the jungle. Appearing from out of the darkness, the illuminated figure of a woman who bears the burden of four sets of arms. The burden, however, does not diminish her beauty. On the contrary, only adds to it.

Kali...

Her hair is long and lush, her skin milky and smooth, her eyes the color of obsidian, her lashes thick and soft. She wears gold necklaces and many bracelets on all eight wrists. The jewelry jangles musically with every fluid motion of her fingers, hands, and arms, as if she were a jellyfish propelling herself along in a clear, calm, deep, blue sea.

In one of her hands, she holds a severed head. Elizabeth's head. In another hand, she holds a sword, of which the wide blade is blood-stained. In yet another hand, she holds Elizabeth's still bleeding heart. I want to scream at the she-devil, reach out and strangle her, but it's impossible to move. I am helpless.

The closer Kali comes to me, the easier it is to make out her face, her naked breasts, her bare belly, the naval pierced with a blue diamond stud. Her arms are never still as they wave and twirl, hypnotizing and frightening me with their macabre dance. When she is finally upon me, she spreads her long legs and straddles me. I enter into her with the length of my manhood and feel her insides as if they've been created not out of human flesh, but lava and flame. It's so hot I want to scream, but I am paralyzed.

"You belong to me, Chase Baker," she whispers softly, but somehow forcefully, passionately.

When I release, she begins to laugh and her face ignites with an intense pleasure that is matched only with my regret, shame, and disgust. She raises herself up and off of me then, and floats away while I fall rapidly back to the earth...a mortal man touched and violated by Satan herself.

WAKE TO A SCREAM, MY BODY ON FIRE, SWEAT-SOAKED.

Anjali raises up, eyes wide. "Chase, am I dreaming?"

I sit up. Listen.

Another shriek.

"Help! Somebody please! Help!" The voice is muffled and distant. But I hear it plain enough.

"You're not dreaming. It's Rudy."

Gazing at my watch. "Holy Christ. It's five in the morning. We've slept all night."

Gathering my gear, I exit the tent, take a quick look around for Rudy. He's nowhere to be seen. I'm holding my automatic, the sweat from my palm coating the grip. To my left, the Sherpas are still asleep.

"Hey!" I bark. "Up, up!"

Both of them wake, raise themselves from the ground.

"Ocha," they recite instinctually. "Ocha."

Behind me, Anjali emerges from the tent.

"Stay here," I say. Then, to the Sherpas, "You come with me."

Another shriek comes from the opposite side of the tree line.

"Tony!" I shout. "Tony, you awake?"

A rustling through the bush and the old excavator appears.

"I heard it," he says, nodding. "Coming from that direction. Not far from the grassy opening where we used the drone last night."

He's holding his automatic.

"Let's go," I bark.

We begin to trudge through the forest, the Sherpas on our tail.

"By the way," I say, "why didn't you wake me to take my turn on watch?"

"Saw you had company."

"You're all heart, Tone." I recall snippets of my nightmare...Kali coming to me...doing something unspeakable to me.

"Well, you know what your old man used to say about you?"

"No, what did the old man say about me?"

"That boy of mine...he's a sucker for the ladies. All they gotta do is smile at him and he's whipped."

"No wonder I'm not married."

"Can't make that crap up, Baker."

We push through the trees and come to the opening. It's then we get our first look at Rudy. He's partially covered by a patch of tall grass, but from what I can see, he's squatting, his pants pulled down around his ankles. Standing four square, maybe fifty feet away, is a black rhino. The two-ton, dinosaur-like beast is snorting through its nostrils, bobbing back and forth on its stubby legs like a boxer warming up in his corner, awaiting that final millisecond when the bell will ring and he comes out charging.

"Rudy," I say from the edge of the woods, "don't move."

"Thanks for the advice, mate," he says in his British accent, his voice filled with quiet panic. "Shoot the thing before he rams me."

I turn to Tony. He's laughing so hard I think he might burst the buttons on his work shirt.

"You think our pistols will bring that thing down?" I say.

"You...need...Bruce's hunting rifle," Tony says in between laughs.

I turn to the Sherpas, relay the order. They run back through the woods to the camp.

"Hold still, Rudy," I say. "Help is coming."

"Hurry it up," he says. "That beast is growing impatient."

"Hey, Rudy," Tony bellows in between chuckles, "you've really got yourself in a shitty situation this time, buddy."

"Shut up, Tony," the bartender says.

"This really stinks, huh?" Tony presses. "You need toilet paper?"

"Tony, shut...up!"

The beast lets out another snort. It takes a few, quick, thunderous steps forward towards Rudy, as if testing the waters.

Rudy screams again.

"Oh shit," Tony says, his voice suddenly deadpan, "this is getting serious."

From where I'm standing, I can see that the blood has drained from Rudy's face and neck, making the red rope burn that rings it even more swollen and painful looking. His blue eyes are open wide and he's blinking rapidly. How the chubby, fifty-something man has been able to hold his body in a squat position for as long as he has is beyond me. Fear is a powerful motivator.

Some rustling coming from behind me. I turn to see the Sherpas returning with the 30.06. They hand me the rifle. Turning to Tony.

"You're the better shot," I say.

He looks at me like I just asked him to shoot his own mother.

"I'm not gonna shoot a beautiful, majestic rhino," he barks. "I'd rather shoot Rudy."

"Holy shit, can you guys please help me now!" shouts Rudy.

"Okay, okay," I say. "I'll do it."

"Go get 'em, Hemingway," Tony says.

"Thanks," I say. "But you're not off the hook that easy. You have to act as my backup in case I miss."

"Why me?"

"Because Sherpas don't shoot, asshole. And you do."

Tony cocks a round into his .9mm, takes a knee, raises it up combat position, takes aim.

I grip the wood stocked hunting rifle in both hands, open the bolt, cock a round into the breach, close the bolt.

"Here I go," I take the first step in my approach to the open space of grassland that separates Rudy from the beast.

I'm no stranger to dangerous situations. I've survived plane crashes, anaconda attacks, and I've even been buried alive. But never in my life have I been made to stare down tons of wild beast that can crush me with its horns in an instant. I'm no expert but from what I've been told by white hunters in the past, a rhino can cover up to twenty meters at a full sprint in just a few seconds. They are far faster than they look.

The animal locks its black eyes on me. He's snorting, bobbing, clawing at the ground with its right hoof. There's no doubt in my mind he's getting ready to charge. Raising the rifle, I press the stock against my shoulder, sight him in, aim for the small sweet fleshy spot above its breast plate but below its neck. Shoot too low and the bullet will lodge itself in the thick, bony material. Shoot too high and the bullet will either pass clean through the neck or, if it lowers its head, which it is sure to do, will simply ricochet off the bony nose.

Inhaling slowly...thumbing off the safety...finger on the trigger...

"Come on, come on, Chase," Tony insists. "He's gonna run you over, man...Do it...Do it now."

"Shoot him, Chase," Rudy whispers hard. "Hell you waiting for, mate."

A droplet of cold sweat drips down into my left eye, rendering it useless

The beast opens up its mouth wide, lets loose with a loud roar. My insides turn to liquid, head begins to spin. I exhale half my air, depress my index finger.

I shoot.

24

THE SHOT MISSES. TOO HIGH.

I cock the rifle again, but the bolt jams.

The rhino yelps, digs in with its front hoofs like a sprinter taking his mark, then explodes in a full frontal charge.

Tony shoots, but also misses.

I back step and, at the same time, make out the sound of Rudy screaming like a girl while he runs away with his pants down around his ankles, falling flat on his face.

Tony fires again and manages to hit the beast in his top horn, the boney material splintering like shrapnel. Forcing back the rifle bolt, I release the jam. Shouldering the weapon once again, I take aim. Fire.

Another miss.

That's when all fear simply pours out of me like

air through a suddenly punctured balloon. Realization fills my veins. I'm about to die. While the sight of a two-ton locomotive with one spear-tipped horn and one now jagged horn coming directly for me fills my vision, I feel almost detached from the earth. Like my body is here, but my soul has already pulled an Elvis and exited the building. Even the rapid-fire gunshots coming from Tony's .9mm don't seem to register. Everything is slowed down and sped up at the same time, like a broken projector.

I close my eyes, await the collision...

...that never happens.

Something else happens instead.

The rhino passes me by entirely. It passes by Rudy. It begins to gallop a big, wide circle around us, all the time snorting and hissing, letting loose with the occasional grunt, like he's much more interested in scaring the crap out of us than killing us. And maybe he is.

After completing two full revolutions, he simply heads for the brush and disappears.

No more rhino.

Tony approaches me, his face a patina of relief and smiles.

Rudy comes up on my opposite side. He's pulling up his pants while he walks.

"Holy crap that was close," he says.

"Exactly," I whisper in disbelief. "Holy...crap."

I'm still in a daze, my body not yet anchored on the solid earth.

"Am I dead?" I say. "And this is it? I gotta spend all eternity with you sons-a-bitches in heaven...or hell?"

Tony laughs aloud, slaps me on the shoulder.

"I can think of worse situations," he says. "But

you're not dead...yet. Although that was one of the bravest things I've ever witnessed, Baker. I have a new respect for you. And to think I used to think of you as the spoiled little daddy's boy. Well, look at you now."

"Tone," I say.

"What is it?"

"I think I peed myself."

He steps back, gingerly. "That's a perfectly normal reaction to facing down a full frontal charge from a fully grown rhino...or so I would imagine."

After a beat, all feeling returns to my limbs. Happily, I discover that I have not peed myself, which makes me feel even prouder. However, it's time we got back on the trail of the God Boy and left this forest behind for good.

"Tony," I say, "let's break camp and get moving." Then, "Rudy, pull up your pants and help the Sherpas with the elephants."

"What about you?" Tony says as he slides a fresh clip into his .9mm.

"I'm going to have a drink," I say. "Or maybe two."

Making my way for the opening in the trees, I head back to camp, hoping that Rudy had the good sense to leave enough whiskey for me.

A HALF HOUR LATER CAMP IS BROKEN, THE TENTS AND equipment packed up and ready for travel. We've mounted our elephants and now are heading in a northwest direction towards Kashmiri's diamond deposit, praying all the time we're not spotted by one of his spies along the way.

The going is slow but steady as the elephants bust through the thickest of foliage with all the powerful efficiency of Abrams battle tanks. At one point, I turn to make an eyeball check on the crew when I see that Rudy's eyes are closing, his head bobbing. The step-and-sway motion of his elephant is putting him to sleep. Meanwhile, Tony is ever alert and vigilant and keeping his eyes open for bandits, his cheek stuffed with fresh tobacco. Anjali has been quiet, and the most we've communicated since waking has been a few casually exchanged smiles. Perhaps she is silently reciting prayers on behalf of her boy.

Here's the truth of the matter: Part of me wants to fall in love with her, but a far bigger part of me knows that I am no good for her. That our *situation* is no good. She's a mom and a good one. A woman who is willing to put her life on the line in order to free her boy. I would do the same for my little girl, in a heartbeat. But something tells me Anjali could never be happy with a vagabond, a wanderer, an explorer. I would only leave her frustrated. And besides, all good love ends badly no matter what form it takes. There's no escaping it.

Or, perhaps I'm thinking too much. Talking myself out of a good thing. A solid and stable thing. Maybe I should give Anjali some credit. She's a big girl. She knows what she's doing. Or maybe like Tony says, I ought to get out of my own way and love the one I'm with. But in the back and fore of my mind, I see the face of Elizabeth as I left her alone on the train platform...as her heart was cut out of her chest by an evil man...

Several hours later, the thick tree cover gives way to a vast open plain.

I order the caravan to stop while I pull out the topo map from the chest pocket on my bush jacket, unfold it. Tony comes up on my right side.

"We're close aren't we?" he says from high atop his elephant, the tusked beast brushing its head lovingly up against the head of my own elephant. Anyone who doesn't believe that elephants are complex, monogamous creatures who aren't evolved enough to love and care for their own, had better think again. How anyone could shoot these glorious creatures for their ivory, or anything else, ought to be shot in the heart by a firing squad.

"We are close," I confirm, as I consult the map along with the GPS coordinates on my smartphone. Then, pressing my index finger against the topo map on what is our exact position, I lock eyes with Tony. "A mile and a half at most," I add. "Once we cross this open field, we enter into another small stretch of woods and then come upon another open plain. That's where we'll find the diamond deposit."

"I'll tell everyone to keep their eyes open," he says before spitting a short stream of black tobacco. Then, turning, "Rudy, wake up for Christ's sake. We're not on vacation."

I turn to see Rudy raise his head up fast.

"I'm awake," he mutters, wiping drool from the side of his mouth.

"Chase," Anjali says, her face filled with anxiety. "I feel my son. I feel he is nearby. Is it true?"

"Not long now," I say.

But one glance at the Sherpas and I can see that they are growing fidgety and nervous. It's like they are perfectly aware the territory they are entering is not only bad, but evil. Even the elephants are getting restless. Sensing that if we don't keep going, I'll lose the confidence of both animal and man, I swing my arm around John Wayne style, shout, "Keep it moving!"

Out on the open plain, the sun beats down on us. I can hear my heart beating in my chest. The elephants grow even more agitated. The air around us seems somehow different. Like some of the oxygen has diminished making breathing more difficult, much more labored. The sky, which had been a brilliant blue, now begins to fill with thick black clouds that swirl as if a tornado funnel is about to emerge from them. The wind picks up, blows coldly and swiftly.

Coming from behind me, the Sherpas are talking in rapid-fire Nepalese. Even with the diamond mine not yet in sight, they are clearly not liking the atmosphere. Can't say that I do either.

"You order up the end of the world, Chase?" Tony barks from the rear.

"Not lately," I say. "But it is a little creepy."

The earth beneath the elephants begins to shake and quake.

"Earthquake," Rudy shouts.

"Chase, I'm afraid," Anjali says as the tremors get worse.

The elephants bend their forelegs, kneel down, and practically toss us off their backs.

"Dismount," I order.

As soon as we've dismounted, the enormous animals rise back up onto tree trunk legs, extend their trunks, and blow out trumpeting wails.

"Grab the stuff," I say, a bad feeling settling into my stomach. "Quick before they run away."

I pull off the 30.06 and my pack. Anjali grabs her pack as well. I can only assume that Tony and Rudy also grabbed their bags, which is a good thing. True to my gut, the elephants turn tail and begin trotting in the opposite direction.

Can't say I blame them.

The tremors are so intense, I have trouble standing upright. It's one thing to be caught out in the open during a major quake, I can only imagine the horror unleashed in overpopulated Kathmandu. The grass burns away and the bare earth beneath it opens up as a hot fire materializes from it. There's a loud wailing while steam heat escapes into the air. Anjali falls on all fours while Tony and Rudy awkwardly make their way to where I'm standing only a few feet away from the now blistered and heaved up earth.

It's then I view an incredible sight. What first appeared to be an earthquake is becoming something else entirely. The shaking ground before us is taking shape. An ovular area about the size of an in-ground swimming pool. The fire isn't randomly spouting out of the openings but is, instead, emerging from out of four distinct holes that have formed in the grass-covered earth. Two eyes, a nose, and a mouth. The earth has formed a giant face that seems as if it were delivered from hell itself. The face resembles the face that formed above the diamond mine when Elizabeth was murdered. I'm standing not far from the mouth when flames spit out of it.

...Kali...you are alive...you are trying to stop us in our tracks before we even come close to the diamond mine...

A great scream comes from down inside the earth. So loud it makes my teeth chatter. The fire that came from the face dies, and in its place something else arises from the four openings.

Anjali comes up on my side.

"What is that black stuff?" she says, her tone urgent and afraid.

"Hey," Rudy says, "it's oil. We're bloody rich."

I take a closer look. "That's not oil."

"Then what is it?" Tony says.

"Those are snakes. Black snakes, rising out of the earth, and covering the ground like a plague."

The Sherpas shriek at the sight, about-face, and begin to run away in the direction of the elephants.

"Our guides are abandoning us," Anjali warns.

"It's what Kali wants!" Tony shouts. "He wants us to turn tail and run."

"That would be a *she*, Tone," I say. Then, "What we have to do, we have to do on our own. Grab your stuff and let's get the hell out of here. To the trees. Now!"

The earth stops shaking, but the snakes keep coming from the face formed in the earth. An evil face that is surely a sign we should stay away from Kashmiri's diamond mine. The warning doesn't come from God. Far from it. The warning comes, instead, from Hell's eternal wrath.

26

WE MAKE A RUN FOR THE TREES. WE DON'T STOP UNTIL
we reach the treeline where we collapse onto our
backs in exhaustion.

"It's good to get away sometimes, ain't it?" Rudy
says. "You know, a little rest and relaxation, fresh air,
and exercise. Five-star hotels and room service. Free
drinks all around and man oh man that breakfast
buffet. I could really get used to this kind of traveling."

"Very funny," Tony says. "You missed your
calling."

"Huddle up everyone," I say. "This is where things
get serious."

I catch the expression on Anjali's face. It couldn't
be more serious if it were chiseled out of granite.

I say, "I want everyone to stick together. Don't
wander off. Keep your eyes and ears open for booby

160

traps. This narrow strip of forest is the last line of cover between us and Kashmiri's compound. I have no idea what to expect, which means anything could happen."

Turning to Rudy. "That means you, pal."

He's got this tight as all hell expression on his round face like a big part of him wants to run away along with the elephants and Sherpas, forget about having any part in rescuing the God Boy. But I know he has his own agenda in mind.

"Sure hope the diamonds are worth it, Chase," he says.

I, too, am feeling the pressure. I'm no stranger to supernatural events. But an evil power like Kali...a power that has the ability to invade my brain while I sleep...is entirely foreign to me. It's not so much being afraid because fear I can deal with. It's more a matter of not knowing what to expect. But then, that's the essence of adventure, isn't it? Not knowing what lies in wait for you.

The jungle is dark and foreboding even midday. Monkeys jump from tree branch to tree branch while giant vampire bats fly away from us in packs of hundreds, or even thousands. Animals don't like earthquakes any more than we do. There isn't much of a trail to follow, so we're forced to bushwhack our way without the assistance of a machete. The going is slow and tough, and our bodies are covered in sweat.

After an hour of hiking, the woods thin out and the grassy plain becomes visible through the breaks in the trees and foliage. There it is, a sight for sore eyes.

Kasmiri's encampment and the diamond deposit.

We look out onto the encampment while hidden by the bush. Trucks and 4X4s circle the many-acred operation. Dozens of slaves have formed an assembly line from the mouth of the tunnel that is housed by the tin-roofed shack. The line of slaves extends to the outside where they dump the contents of their overloaded wheel barrels onto the motorized screens which then sift the rocks and gravel for pieces of priceless diamonds. By all appearances, the earthquake hasn't had any effect on the mining operation as if it was built to withstand a seismic event.

Every now and again one of the many black-robed Thuggees who guard the place fires off a round or two in the air to keep the assembly line moving as rapidly as possible.

"Tony," I say, "binoculars."

The excavator pulls them from around his neck, hands them to me. I put them to my eyes and grab my first close-up view.

"Four soldiers guard the tunnel opening and the shack that surrounds it," I say. "Another four to six are walking the perimeter of the exposed diamond deposit. The Kali statue has gone underground since last night's ceremony."

I feel the key hanging from the leather strap around my neck. It's not only crucial that I get to that boy. I need to get at that statue to unlock it. To find out its secret. A secret that, in my mind, could mean the end of the line for the resurrected Kali.

"We could just shoot them," Tony says.

"Once we drop the first man, the rest will spill out of that hole in the ground like that plague of snakes we saw back there."

"Good point," Tony says. "Best to go with our original plan. Wait until dark, plug up the air intakes, force them out by suffocation."

"Does that mean we've got to wait?" Anjali asks.

"We need the cover of darkness," I say. "Without decent firepower, we're as good as doomed."

Rudy shuffles closer to me.

"You mean I gotta go all night without a drink?" he says. "That ain't right."

"Sorry, Rudy," I say. "Look at it this way. It'll do you liver good."

He makes a sour face. "Stuff I gotta go through to get rich."

I pull out my .45, release the clip, check the load.

"Everyone make an inventory of their weapons," I say. "Something tells me we'll need every last round."

I'm just about to return the piece to my shoulder holster when I feel the solid metal gun barrel pressed against the back of my head.

27

SO MUCH FOR OUR PLAN OF CUNNING, STEALTH, AND plugging up the air intakes.

The new breed of 21st century Thuggees bind our hands behind our backs with good old fashioned duct tape. They scream orders in Hindi and Nepali. Words that mean nothing to me. But that doesn't mean I don't feel their punches to my gut. To my head.

The man I pick out as the Captain of the Guard is as big and tall as a giant. He's got a thick, black beard and mustache, and he bears a black half-moon tattoo of the Thuggee on his forehead. Wrapped around his waist is a wide yellow sash with a large medallion planted in its center. If my history serves me correct, the Thuggee were famous for utilizing the scarf as a garrote—a device by which they would torture their captives by strangulation and/or flogging.

I hope my history serves me wrong.

"Anjali," I whisper. "You okay?"

"I'm okay, Chase," she says. "Just do as they say. These men aren't interested in quick kills. They will torture you first."

"Silence!" Black Beard shouts. "There will be no talking."

...*So the big man speaks English...maybe like a lot of terrorists, he was educated in the States*...

"Sir," Rudy interjects. "Sir, allow me to explain. This isn't what you think."

"Rudy, shut up," Tony says.

But the bartender barrels his way for Black Beard like he has no business being his captive.

"Please allow me to explain," Rudy presses. "You see, I have no idea who these people are. I was only out for a hike when I came across them after that dreadful earthquake. If you let me go, I can get you money. Lots of it. I promise."

"Traitor," Tony says.

"We should have let him hang," I say.

"So, what do you say?" Rudy presses to Black Beard. "Let me go and I'll fetch..."

Raising his fist, Black Beard brings it down upon Rudy's head, knocking him cold. But the bartender comes back around when Black Beard tosses half the water from his canteen onto his chubby face. From down on the jungle floor, Rudy shakes his head, looks around. "Where am I?"

"Things are definitely not looking up," Tony says.

"Couldn't agree more," I say.

"That monster tried to scramble my brains," Rudy mumbles.

"Silence!" Black Beards repeats.

The Thuggees collect our weapons and begin to

march us across the grassy plain, all the time poking us with the barrels of their automatic rifles until we come to the tin shack protected entrance to the tunnel. Two solid steel doors secure the entry. But for now anyway, the doors are wide open while slaves move in and out with their wheel barrels of diamond-studded earth along a concrete ramp that steadily descends into the earth.

Rudy perks up as soon as he sees the wheel barrels being dumped onto the screens, some of the crystal clear diamonds automatically separated from the worthless earth, others not so bright and still embedded in chunks of rock.

"Look at that," he whispers. "I can bet that each one of those wheel barrels represents a million Pounds."

Obviously his head isn't hurting anymore.

"You will follow," Black Beard insists.

"Like we have a choice," I say, as the guard behind me once more pokes me in the spine with the barrel of his Kalashnikov.

We're led into the tunnel entrance where we immediately hook a left down an empty corridor made of reinforced concrete and illuminated with ceiling-mounted lamps protected behind metal cages. These guys aren't kidding around. The floor descends at a thirty-five-degree angle which means our descent is rather rapid, and just to prove it, the air becomes cooler, moister with each step we take.

After maybe fifteen minutes of walking, the newly constructed tunnel empties out into a large, ancient space that appears to have been carved out of stone centuries ago. We're made to stand shoulder to shoulder and not make a move. Before us is a kind of Hindu temple that's been sculpted into the opposing rock face. It must be one hundred feet high by at least that wide in length. Carved into the center of the façade, above the door, is an eight-armed Kali, its eyes wide open gazing down upon us, its tongue protruding from its mouth mocking us, a sword in one hand and a severed head in another, beating hearts in the others. Old fashion fire-lit torches hang from the walls beside the thick stone doors. This must be the temple that was constructed to honor Kali. A temple built far underground and nearly impossible to find. Until Elizabeth finally discovered it.

"What the hell is this?" Rudy says. "The temple of doom?"

Black Beard turns, peers at Rudy with his black eyes. "You are alive, only because Kashmiri wants it that way. Do you understand?"

Eyes wide, Rudy swallows, his Adams apple bobbing up and down in his neck like a frightened turkey facing a sharpened axe. Just then, the big doors to the temple begin to tremble as they slowly open.

"Easy everyone," I say. "Keep cool."

A man emerges from the opening. He's tall, slim, and bearing a beard that's just as black and thick as Black Beard's. He's also wearing a green military-issue jacket, and aviator sunglasses, even inside this dimly lit, Hollywood-like setup.

Kashmiri...The son of a bitch who cut out Elizabeth's heart...

"My guests have arrived," he says, working up a smile.

He approaches us. First he eyes me, then moving down the line, Tony, and after him, Rudy. When he comes to Anjali, he raises his hand. My pulse begins to pound in my temples because I'm convinced he is about to wrap his fingers around her neck. But he does no such thing. Instead, he gently places his hand to her face, leans in, kisses her gently on the mouth.

"Anjali," he says, "you should never have come here. I forbade it." Setting his hands on her shoulder. "But oh, how I've missed you so."

"Kashmiri," she says. "I thought I'd never see you again."

I'M NOT SURE WHY I'M SO SURPRISED THAT KASHMIRI
and Anjali have a past. Or should I say, surprised they
share a past, present, and future. What should also
come as no surprise is that she used me to lead her
here. Maybe she should have simply texted Kashmiri
and he could have flown her out here on his own. Or
perhaps that would have been the wrong approach.
Judging by what Kashmiri said, Anjali was forbidden
to come here. Makes sense if he's kidnaped her son.
But then, maybe Kashmiri is the real father. Maybe
that's what this little kidnaping of the God Boy is all
about. Maybe using him as a conduit to summon up
Kali is simply the family biz. Or maybe my
imagination is going whacky.

"Give me a good reason why I shouldn't send you
away, Anjali," Kashmiri says as he leads us to the far

end of the large room where he keeps a desk, "and kill all of your friends while I'm at it."

"Mr. Kashmiri," Rudy says, taking a step forward. "Allow me to introduce myself. My name is Rudy Valenty, and I am at your service. From the looks of it, you have quite the diamond drilling operation going on here, and I just happen to be an expert diamond sales executive from—"

Black Beard reaches out, backhands Rudy across the face. The slap is so powerful it nearly knocks him on his back.

"Get back," Black Beard insists. "No talking."

"No talking," a dazed Rudy whispers under his breath. "No talking...No...Talking..."

"He's got the key," Anjali says, as her wrists are unbound and she takes her place beside Kashmiri where he's now seated behind a great desk carved out of mahogany. "The one who thinks he's Indiana Jones. He's got the key that will unlock the Kali statue and reveal her secrets."

Anjali knows the key will not reveal secrets so much as kill Kali once the statue is unlocked. Maybe she's not so in love with Kashmiri after all. Maybe she's not double-crossing us but only playing the situation like she's double-crossing us...No choice but to calm down and wait to see how it all plays out...

I can't help but notice that only one item occupies the desktop. It's an old half-moon shaped dagger with worn leather surrounding the grip. No guns for Kashmiri the Thuggee terrorist. The man is strictly old school.

"Indiana Jones...now that hurts," I say. "I always thought of myself as Ernest Hemingway meets Antoine de Saint-Exupéry."

I'm fighting the duct tape that binds my wrists

together. It's a tight fit, but I've been in enough hands-tied-behind-my-back situations to know that stitching a pen knife blade to the interior of one's belt, the razor sharp edge facing outwards, is the prudent thing to do. I've also practiced the technique of sawing away at whatever means the bad guys choose to bind me with, be it rope or duct tape, without their having the slightest clue. Like the two armed bandits standing behind me by the door of this dimly lit room, for example. It's a matter of standing at an angle where they simply don't notice what I'm doing with my fingers.

"What key?" Rudy says. Then, catching himself. "Oh, yes, of course. *That* key."

Kashmiri turns, focuses in on Rudy.

"Who did this man say he was again?" he says.

"He's the mastermind behind this whole thing," Tony says. "It's him you wanna torture."

"Are you kidding me?" Rudy screams. "Until an hour ago, I'd never seen these people in my life. I'm a citizen of Her Majesty's Great Britannia and I demand to be released at once." He smiles. "Then perhaps we'll discuss the key and its location. For a price of course."

"Gag this man," Kashmiri says to Black Beard. The big, black-turbaned man nods to one of the armed Thuggee bandits who immediately approaches Rudy, rips a considerable piece of duct tape from its roll, and attaches it to his chubby face, from ear lobe to ear lobe.

Kashmiri's sunglasses-shielded eyes back on me.

"Harbans," he says. "I want you to extract the truth from Mr. Baker regarding the true whereabouts of the key."

Black Beard/Harbans removes his sash, twirls it around in his two hands so that it forms a thick rope with a solid metal pendant at the end. He approaches me, cocks the sash back as if it were a whip, and readies to strike me with it. But that's when I hear, "Stop!"

It's Anjali.

She comes around Kashmiri's desk.

"Allow me, Kashmiri," she says, removing the half-moon-shaped dagger off of the desk. "I believe I know precisely how to get Mr. Baker to reveal the location of the key. Then, once I produce it, you may tend to him as you wish." She laughs. "What's left of him, that is."

"Be quick, Anjali," he says. "We must start our ceremony soon. Maybe you have come here against my wishes. But now that you are here, I would very much like you to be a part of it." He scans the rest of us with his sunglass shielded eyes. "In fact, I shall very much enjoy having you all as my guests at the ceremony."

...*Another Thuggee ceremony...another sacrifice to Kali...no doubt all three of us fit the bill as sacrificial lambs...*

Anjali comes to me, blade gripped in her hand. She looks me in the eye.

"Now, Mr. Baker," she says, pressing the tip of the knife against the underside of my chin. So hard the pain shoots up into my face, behind my eyeballs. "Where is the key?"

"Don't do it, Chase," Tony says over my right shoulder. "They're gonna kill us anyway. Don't give the broad the satisfaction."

Coming from the left, Rudy is screaming something into his gag.

She starts touching me all over like she's patting me down. And she is. When she comes to my right side leg pocket on my jungle green cargo pants, she unbuttons it, reaches inside like she's convinced the key is located there. But she knows full well the key is strung around my neck and hidden behind the T-shirt beneath my work-shirt. She removes her hand from my pocket, holds it up with fingers spread as if to demonstrate just how empty it is. Looking up at me, she issues me a wink of her left eye. Not much of wink. Nothing anyone in the know would think twice about. But a wink all the same. She's playing both sides and doing so with great effectiveness. Maybe even buying us precious time.

She makes a complete search of all my pockets and finishing up by peering down inside my black T-shirt.

"Did you wanna see up my ass too?" I say, finally feeling the sweet release of my duct taped wrists.

She smiles. "I'm sure that won't be necessary, Mr. Baker." Turning to Kashmiri. "The key is not on him."

"Then we will have Harbons take care of him," the Islamist terrorist turned Thuggee chieftain insists. "Perhaps he hid it somewhere inside the jungle and now it is just waiting there to be found."

Harbons grabs my arm with his iron grip. But that's when Anjali steps forward, drives the dagger into the monster's side.

"Chase run!" she screams.

Harbons falls.

Pulling my hands apart, I turn quick and swift kick the guard on the right in the balls. Tony makes like a bull and rams the other guard with his head, driving him back against the stone wall. Meanwhile, Rudy steps forward, kicks the first guard's AK-47 out of his hands, so that it lands on the stone floor, slides towards the door.

"Anjali, get Tony's wrists," I bark while going for the automatic rifle. Picking it up, I turn and see that Kashmiri has jumped over his desk and taken cover behind it. I trigger a short burst of rounds into it. But that's when the second guard raises his rifle. Anjali is quicker and runs the blade across his neck, sending a spout of arterial blood against the wall.

"And yet another surprise for the Catholic girl," I say. "You're a little too good with a knife."

"By the grace of God, I go," she barks.

Kashmiri stands then, an automatic gripped in his shooting hand. He fires, the round ricocheting against the stone wall. I spray his desk once more and he catches a round in the upper left thigh, dropping him on the spot.

Anjali cuts Tony's wrists free. He picks up a second AK, and we make for the open door. But that's when Rudy jumps ahead of us. He's wide-eyed and panicked.

"Oh Christ," I say. "Cut him loose and get out."

"You can't run!" Kashmiri shouts. He quickly changes clips and shoots at will, the rounds whizzing past my head, ricocheting against the stone wall. "You are surrounded on all sides. We will torture you, rip out your hearts, and feed them to Kali. Do you hear me!?!"

I return fire, but he's once more taking cover behind the desk. I turn back towards the door.

"Just give me one clean shot, asshole," I say. But no one can hear me above the noise of the gunfire.

I search for Anjali. She's cutting Rudy's tape. When he's free, I shout, "Let's just go while we have the chance!"

Kashmiri fires again.

This time, I don't bother with returning fire.

Instead, the four of us head back out into the open space, closing the wood doors behind us. Pulling one of the torches off the wall, I stuff it into the openers, securing both doors and locking Kashmiri inside.

For how long, only Kali knows.

WE STAND IN SILENCE OUTSIDE THE GREAT WOOD temple doors until I make out the sound of movement. The unmistakable sound of stone splitting. Something only a digger will recognize immediately.

"You hear that, Chase?" Tony says. "Something's giving way down here."

"Yeah," I say. "But where's it coming from?"

I look all around me. But the louder the harsh noise gets, the more my internal radar begs me to look up. That's when I see her. The life-sized stone carving of Kali, coming alive, tearing herself from the wall. The stone Kali drops down from the wall, lands on her two feet with an earth-pounding thud. In one of her many hands, she grips a crescent-shaped sword.

"That isn't real," Rudy screams. Out the corner of my eye, I see him close his eyes. "It's not real," he chants. "It's not real...It's not real...Wake up, Rudy. Wake up, Rudy. Wake up..."

She waves her arms with great agility like they are made of flesh and bone and not stone. The big blade slices through the air, barely missing my head. I stumble backward while she swings the blade again, knocking the AK-47 from my hands.

I regain my balance while Kali repositions herself, attempting to separate me from the rest of the gang by standing between us.

"Tony," I say, "plant a bead on her while I distract her."

The old excavator shoulders the AK while I back-step slowly, the stone monster following, as planned. That's when her eyes go wide, her mouth opening and a scream emerging from it that's so loud it feels as if it's piercing my eardrums.

She swings the blade at my head, but I'm able to duck in time, dropping to my knees.

"Now, Tony!" I shout. "Send her back to hell!"

Tony opens up with his Kalishnikov, the rounds shattering the stone figure into a dozen pieces which quickly scatter away on their own into the recesses of the underground chamber.

"Let's get the hell out of here before that Kali freak pulls a Humpty Dumpty and puts herself back together again," Tony says.

Rudy slowly opens his eyes. "Is she gone?"

"She's gone," I say, standing, gathering up the firearm Kali knocked out of my hands. "Thanks for the help. Now let's get the hell out of here."

"But what about my son?" Anjali begs. "Where can he possibly be?"

"That's the question, isn't it?" I say, pivoting on the balls of my feet, giving the wide open chamber the once over. But what I really want to do right now is ask

Anjali how she so innocently happens to know Kashmiri. But there's no time for that. On second thought. "So how did you and that terrorist get so chummy? Guess you forgot to mention that little tidbit of information."

She looks at me with her deep, dark eyes.

"Yeah, nice work, lady," Tony says. "For a second there, I thought we were supper for Kali. I was already counting on how good it would feel to tear your eyeballs out."

"It's not as it appears, Chase," she says. "Kashmiri and I became lovers for a brief time after Singh left me. I truly had no idea he was a terrorist because he only visited me once a month and only at our humble house in Varanasi. He referred to himself as a freedom fighter. That was the extent of it. Something not at all unusual for that area of the world. But you see, he took a great and, what seemed at the time, loving interest in Rajesh. He became like a father to the boy when no one wanted anything to do with him, gifting him with food, clothing, and money even long after we stopped being lovers.

"But then, one day I awoke to find the boy gone. This was not long after Rajesh began proving his saintliness by performing miracles and attracting large crowds of believers. That Kashmiri was behind the abduction, there was no doubt. Only then did I discover the truth about his terrible past. About his terrorist activities with the 313 in Pakistan."

"Ha," Rudy says, "a likely story, lady."

"Well, it's one we're gonna have to go with for now," I say, as I desperately look around for a way out of this place. An alarm is sounding and the sound of jack boots descending into the tunnel echoes down into this chamber.

"The devils are descending, Chase," Tony says.

"Why didn't that Kali defend Kashmiri?" says Rudy. "Why wait until we step out of his office to attack us? Shouldn't she have at least made a guest appearance inside the office? Maybe made the floor open up beneath our feet or something?"

"My guess is Kali has to be summoned to do that," I say. "What happened out there in the jungle...the face appearing in the ground. The fire and the snakes. And what just happened inside this chamber...Kashmiri is somehow able to summon the devil in short bursts only."

"We must find a way out of here," Anjali insists. "Before one of those short bursts of evil turns into a far too long one."

Pounding coming from inside the big wood doors. Rifle stocks against the wood slabs. Kashmiri and some of his men trying like hell to get out...only a matter of seconds until they succeed.

The flames of the wall-mounted torch and the one I stuck into the door openers are flickering like there's a breeze blowing inside the big chamber. I recall what Tony said about air vents feeding oxygen into the underground depths and venting the bad CO_2 out.

"Spread out everybody," I say. "Check the walls for an opening. There's got to be a way out of here."

"Maybe we should go back into Kashmiri's office," Rudy suggests.

The sound of boot-steps getting louder as the Thuggees descend the ramp.

"There's no time for that," I insist. "Besides, the first person who steps through that door is a dead man. There's got to be an opening and it's got to be here."

"Why?" Tony says.

"Because, I damn well say so," I spit.

The boot-steps sound like their only a few feet away, the Thuggees shouting, screaming for blood. The pounding on the wood doors is getting more intense. Then comes multiple gunshots. Bullets bursting through the wood, the torch that holds the openers together bending, about to snap in half, the flame spreading from the torch head, igniting the dry wood doors.

I go to the section of wall where I suspect the breeze is originating from and begin to examine it. Crouching, I feel the wall's surface with the palms of my hands and my fingertips.

Anjali comes to me then. Tears are falling from her big eyes.

"We search in vain, Chase," she says, pressing her back to the stone wall. "We're as good as dead."

That's when Anjali disappears.

RATHER, ANJALI DOESN'T DISAPPEAR SO MUCH AS SHE accidentally uncovers a secret passage hidden in the stone wall.

"Hey," Rudy says. "Where'd she go?"

I place my hands on the exact spot where Anjali slipped through the rabbit hole and, after a few carefully placed shoves, the solid rock door spins open on its vertically mounted hinges.

"Well, I'll be dipped," Tony says. "This *is* a Hollywood set."

I hold the door for the two men as they enter into the dark corridor. Standing a few feet away, her back to me, is Anjali.

"Chase," she says, turning to me. "Do you hear that?"

"Hear what?" I say, shouldering the AK-47 by its leather belt.

I allow the stone door to close on its own.

"Everyone quiet," I order.

Taking a step into the corridor, I listen intently. Along with the distinct odor of human sweat, I hear the clanging of metal against metal and metal against rock. I hear voices wailing, crying. I hear something cracking. Short, sharp, cracking. Like the crack of a whip. I add it all up inside my brain.

"This leads to the heart of the diamond mine," I say.

Rudy lights up at the news. He starts looking around.

"I need a shopping bag," he says. "Anyone got a plastic shopping bag? I'm not leaving here without my retirement etched in brilliant stone, so to speak."

"Take it easy, Rudy," Tony says. "Our first priority is finding Anjali's kid, our second priority is getting out of here alive."

"Let's go, everyone," I say, my eyes focused on the dim light that seems to be coming from the mine at the end of what I estimate to be a one hundred meter corridor.

We walk, eyes wide open, at the ready, just in case we're heading into a trap. But my guess is that this passage serves a distinct purpose other than doing damage to those who tread its stone floor. My guess is that this is a secret corridor for a man like Kashmiri to make a check on the progress of the work being conducted by his band of slave laborers in the mine.

When we come to the end of the corridor, my suspicion rings true. The corridor empties into a small observational area also hewn out of the cave bedrock. There are three distinct round windows carved into a short wall that looks out on a massive mine. My heart nearly skips a beat when I get my first good look at what lies below. All breath escapes my lungs. I've never seen anything like it in my life. One thing is now for certain. The legend of the great India diamond mine is absolutely true. But the reason it hasn't been located in India is because it's in Nepal, outside the fenced-in perimeter of the Chitwan National Forest. No wonder it's eluded explorers for centuries.

"Easy everyone," I say. "Don't let anyone see your face."

The operation is enormous. The mine isn't only comprised of countless chunks of diamonds embedded in the granite walls. It also houses in its core a behemoth blue diamond that must be as big as a two-story house.

"My God in heaven above," Anjali exhales. "I've never seen anything so beautiful surrounded by something so ugly."

The blue diamond glows in the fire and electric lamplight as though it contains its own electric charge. And perhaps it does. One thing it houses inside a core opening at its very top is the Golden Kali Statue. The Ancient Hindus must have possessed the know-how to drill a hole deep enough into the blue diamond to house the statue, then rigged up a mechanical winch system that would raise it up during the ceremonial processionals. Or, maybe the power discharged by the diamond itself is enough to raise the statue.

"How do we get down there?" Rudy asks. "The only thing keeping me from being rich beyond my wildest dreams is standing here doing nothing."

"Rudy," Tony says, "you go down there now, you'll be shot on the spot."

"Tony's right," I say. "The Thuggees are crawling all over the joint. You'll never make it."

There must be three hundred slaves chopping away at the walls with hydraulic chisels and lightweight jackhammers. Some use old-fashioned picks and iron bars to free the little chunks of diamond. Working alongside them are the wheel barrel men who are forced to push the overloaded barrels up a ramp made of wood plank-topped scaffolding that winds its way around the entire mine perimeter.

Out the corner of my eye, I catch a particularly thin and weak man who is pushing his wheel barrel up the incline. Problem is, his strength is running out. He's barely half way up when his wheel barrel tips, dumping the contents out onto the rocky floor below. One of the black-robed bandits jogs up to the sick looking slave, shoulders his Kalashnikov and shoots him on the spot.

The shot reverberates across the entire mine, causing everyone to stop what they're doing, if only for a few brief seconds. That's when the source of the gunshot is revealed. Some of the Thuggees remove their red sashes, spin them like you would a towel, and with the little metal pendant attached to the very tip, savagely whip the exposed backs of the slaves until the flesh opens up and bleeds.

Maybe I don't understand Nepalese or any of the Indian dialects. But I don't have to know the language to realize they are shouting at the slaves to get back to work. Get back to work...or die.

I turn back to the others.

"You got a plan?" Tony says.

"It's not much," I say, cocking the AK-47, "but at least we have the element of surprise."

"Chase," Anjali says, worry painting her face, "perhaps we should rethink this. You can get killed going in there like a Wild West cowboy."

"You'd be surprised how effective an all-out frontal assault can be."

"You do what you have to," says Rudy, setting down his rifle. "And I'm going to do what I have to do. All I ask is that you let me do my thing first."

"Rudy," Tony says. "Just what in the hell do you think you're doing?"

"Utilizing stealth to my advantage," the barkeep says, pulling off his shirt, then his boots and finally his pants so that he's wearing nothing but baggy blue boxer shorts inscribed with little skulls and crossbones. "I'm going to slip in alongside one of those poor slaves, fill me a wheel barrel full of fortune and fame, and then I'm going to simply walk out of this creepy place, a very wealthy man."

"Way to help out with our cause of reuniting a mother with her son," Tony says, acid in his tone and on his pursed lips.

"One for Rudy," says the bartender while rolling up his clothing in a ball, tucking it under his arm, "and all for Rudy. That's what I say."

Anjali shakes her head in disbelief.

"Do what you gotta do, Rudy," I say, "But be quick about it."

"You're going to let him try and get away with this, Chase?" Anjali says.

"Don't worry," I say. "Rudy is a survivor. Isn't that right, Rudy?"

He grins likes he's already rich, the process of digging up a few gems merely a minor inconvenience.

"You got that right, Mr. Chase. Sorry things didn't work out the way you wanted them to. But then, them's the breaks."

Climbing up the short wall over the three portholes, he then makes the descent on the other side and slowly shimmies his way along the angled side of the crevice and into the diamond pit. I have to give him credit, because he manages to do so quickly and without alarm so that within a few seconds, he's blended in with the hundreds of half-naked slaves, filling up his own wheel barrel with chunks of rock he's removing from the quarry with a pickaxe.

A full minute goes by before one of the Thuggee bandits spots him.

"Okay guys," I say, "this is our cue. Maybe Rudy thinks he's gone rogue, but he's actually providing us with an invaluable service. He's providing us with a distraction."

"Lock and load," Tony says, cocking his AK47, then stuffing some chew inside his cheek.

"May the good Lord watch over us," Anjali says, pulling back the slide on her .9mm.

"On three," I say.

I start counting. Before the sound of the number three has exited my lips, we're over the wall.

A PAIR OF GUARDS ARE ABOUT TO POUNCE ON RUDY
when I line them up in my sights, shoot them dead.
The Thuggee might appear terrifying and
indestructible as all hell in their black robes, hoods,
masked faces, revealing only black eyes filled with
hate, but their skin and flesh are just as fragile as
anyone else's. And when they drop dead, they look
very dead and the frightening exterior they once
possessed only a few moments before now appear
comic as their bodies and limbs contort spastically
under their own weight.

But they keep coming at us, which is what I want
as Tony and I cut them down one by one. Anjali acts
as a kind of Gunga Din, stealing weapons and ammo
from the dead and feeding them to us as fast as we
can shoot them. It takes me a moment to relocate him,

but when I do, I see Rudy doing something that defies all logic. Still dressed in nothing but his boxer shorts, he is wheeling a wheel barrel full of gravel and diamonds up the ramp, the bullets whizzing past his head as if they were nothing more than harmless mosquitoes.

"Rudy!" I scream. "Get down! Go back!"

But all he sees are dollar signs dancing around his head. Nothing is going to prevent him from becoming a man rich beyond his wildest dreams. But when a Kalashnikov-armed Thuggee, who's making his way down the ramp, spots the bartender trying to make off with the loot, he triggers a long burst that nearly splits Rudy in two at the waist. Despite the wounds, Rudy somehow manages to take a couple of more steps while pushing the wheel barrel, as if his brain has not yet registered the fact that not only is wealth beyond his wildest dreams going to elude him, so is living. His body, along with the contents of the wheel barrel, falls over the side of the ramp onto the pit floor below.

Glancing at Tony, I can see his face go tight as a tick, his eyes wide. Rudy was his friend. Sure, Rudy wasn't much of a team player, but you don't shoot one of Tony's friends and not pay for it. He grabs hold of a second AK47 and begins shooting two-fisted into the sea of Thuggees, firing from the hip, Rambo-style, screaming at the top of his lungs. It's a massacre as the Thuggees drop dead, one after the other, some of them falling on top of one other.

The slaves are quick to notice that their captures are losing not only the battle but the war. Slowly, they emerge from whatever cover they can find and begin to toss rocks at the Thuggees. Some of the slaves attack the bandits with their pickaxes and others use their shovels, letting loose with a rage and vengeance that's been pent up for weeks and months. When the slaves are able to steal some weapons, they begin to shoot the Thuggees down with all the efficiency of mining diamonds from the diamond mine. The spontaneous slave revolt is so successful that Tony and I are able to cease fire.

"Let's go get the boy," I say to Anjali, shouldering my weapon.

Spotting one of the slaves who is firing upon the now retreating Thuggee, I pull him aside.

"Speak English?" I say.

He bears the sweat and dirt-covered concave-cheeked face of a man who is starving, but his eyes are filled with happiness and revenge. I ask him where they keep the God Boy...the boy with six arms. Surely he knows of the boy.

He raises his right hand, points to a place at the top of the pit, not far from where the ramp meets the exit corridor.

He says, "At the top of the ramp you will see a steel door embedded in the wall. They keep the child in there. But you will not be able to get inside without a key." He pauses. Then, "But I know something that might help you."

He makes his way back down into the pit and, slipping both his hands under the robe of a dead Thuggee, comes back with three sticks of dynamite.

"Use these," he says.

"Old school," I say.

But he just shakes his head like he doesn't understand my meaning.

"Anjali, let's go," I say. Then, looking around for Tony, I finally locate him. He's kneeling over Rudy, where the bartender landed beside the ramp.

"Tony," I say, "we've got to move."

But he raises his hand, waves me off, like he needs to make peace with his friend first. After a moment that seems like an hour, he sets the same hand onto Rudy's eyes and closes them. Standing, he walks away from Rudy for the final time and without a word, begins the climb up the ramp.

AT THE TOP OF THE RAMP, WE COME TO THE LONG corridor that leads out through the still open steel doors. To our left is a small alcove. Planted in the center of the far wall is a solid metal door that's been padlocked. There's no window embedded in the door so it's impossible to make a visual on the God Boy.

"Anjali," I say, "we have to blow the door and do it now."

"What if he is injured in the blast?" she says, ever the concerned mother.

"Chance we gotta take," I say. "But maybe you can speak to him through the door, warn him of what's coming."

Anjali approaches the door, presses her ear to it, as if listening for a sign of life. The look on her face is both desperation and joy. The emotions fight one another. On one hand, she is convinced her son is being held against his will on the opposite side of this steel door, and on the other, there's the chance of him either being hurt or ill or both. Perhaps he is even dead. The only way to know what to expect is to get him out of there as quickly and safely as possible.

"Rajesh," she says sternly. "This is your mother. I have come for you. If you can hear me, I need you to get away from the door. There is going to be a loud explosion and then the door is going to fall off. Do you understand me?" She then repeats the same words in her native tongue, as though speaking to her child in two different languages will make him understand without question, the importance of his being nowhere near the door when it blows.

Pulling one of the sticks of dynamite from my waistband, I fit it into the U-shaped clasp on the padlock. Then, reaching into the left chest pocket on my bush jacket, I retrieve my Bic lighter.

"Stand back," I say, lighting the fuse.

The three of us exit the alcove out into the hall, where we step away from the opening, pressing our backs against the stone wall. The explosion is loud, fiery, and powerful. It seems as if the entire diamond quarry is shaken loose.

Spinning around, we head back through the opening and see that the door has been blown open to reveal a simple room not much bigger than a jail cell. I get my first look at the boy then. The God Boy. He is seated on the stone floor of the windowless room, lotus style. His many arms are open wide, his hands positioned palms upward. He is bare-chested and bare-legged, with only a loin cloth for clothing, and he is sickly thin. His hair is richly black, parted in the center, and so long it drapes his smooth, round face like a silk veil.

Despite the force and suddenness of the explosion, he seems to be caught up in a kind of trance. He might be only five years old and in terrible health, but the energy that he gives off is something I've never before experienced. It is as physical as it is emotional. Maybe there really is something to his being considered a God. Perhaps his physical condition is not just a birth defect, but, in fact, something more. Nepal and India are the lands of reincarnation. Places where death is not an end, but the natural beginning to a new life. Is it possible Rajesh is the reincarnation of one of these Gods? Or am I letting my imagination run away with itself?

...You didn't imagine that stone Kali peeling itself away from the wall, or the giant face of Kali appearing in the quaking earth, or the vaporous image of Kali being summoned when Elizabeth's heart was cut out...You didn't imagine any of it...This isn't fiction like one of your books, Chase...

Anjali goes to her son, drops to her knees before the boy, embraces him by kissing both his cheeks. Tears run down her face as she takes the small boy in her arms, cradles him like he's a newborn. Fact is, he can't weigh more than twenty-five or thirty pounds. Maybe less. She lifts him up off the floor and he smiles at his mother, wrapping his hands around her neck.

"You are safe, Rajesh," she says. "Nothing can happen to you now."

"These men," Rajesh whispers. "These bad men stick needles in me. They make me very, very sleepy, mother."

Tony and I lock eyes.

"They've been drugging him," he says. "Sedating him. Bastards."

193

"Let's just get the hell out of here while we have the chance," I insist.

Pulling the Kalashnikov off my shoulder, I grip it with both hands at the ready. Tony does the same. I step out into the hall to the intermittent sounds of gunfire coming from down in the pit combined with screaming, dying men—most of them Thuggees—I proceed towards the open steel doors.

"Double-time everyone," I say, picking up the pace.

We're not fifty feet from freedom when the doors slam closed, and the electric light in the corridor goes black.

I PULL OUT MY MINI-MAGLITE, SHINE IT ON THE opposite end of the corridor near the alcove and the entrance to the main diamond pit ramp. The pair of steel doors protecting that end of the corridor have also been automatically closed. I shine the light up one end of the corridor and down the other.

"What shall we do, Chase?" Anjali pleads.

"Just stay still," Tony says. "For certain, Kashmiri is listening in. Aren't you Kashmiri, you terrorist bastard?"

Tony's words echo inside the stone and concrete corridor like the Mayday warning on a crashing jetliner.

"I don't like this," he adds, pointing the barrel of his rifle at one set of doors, then pointing it at the other and back again, as if at any second they might open up and release an army of Thuggees to descend upon us. Maybe that's exactly what's about to happen.

But the doors don't open and no bandits pour into the long, narrow space. Instead, something begins to float down from the ceiling like a heavy cloud. Raising the MagLite I can see that a gas is being sprayed into the corridor via a series of spouts mounted to the concrete ceiling.

"They're gassing us," I say while recalling the two additional dynamite sticks shoved into my pant waist. "Head for the doors. We'll blast our way out."

We run as the floor splits down the center and opens up onto a deep, dark, bottomless, black hole.

Opening my eyes, I pull myself back up *onto my feet. I see that I have entered into a second concrete corridor that is dimly illuminated not from electric light, but from something that's positioned at the very end of the corridor. I'm alone. I have no idea where the others have gone. If they are alive or dead. I only know that I'm standing in this long corridor and that I am not afraid.*

Soon the light shifts and the silhouette of a body takes shape. The body comes closer, its footsteps echo on the concrete floor. The closer the person comes, the more I can tell she is a woman. When she is closer still, I can see that she is not just any woman.

She is Elizabeth.

Eyes fill. Heart beats.

"Elizabeth," I say. "I saw you..."

She raises her hand, smiles, brings her fingers as close as she can to my lips without actually touching them.

"I know what you saw," she says. "I felt your presence when it happened. I knew you were close."

"But not close enough."

"That's my fault. I left you, remember? At the train station."

I look her up and down. Her hair is clean and long, parted neatly on the side. She's wearing a clean, black, T-shirt and a pair of green cargo pants, leather Cleopatra sandals on her feet. She looks like she's never been healthier. Even her toenails are painted a light shade of red.

"But I never stopped loving you," I say. "I never stopped thinking about you."

"I never stopped loving you either, Chase. But I knew I would never be happy until I located the statue. And finally, I did."

"Are you happy now?"

She cocks her head over her shoulder.

"That's a very good question," she says bright eyed. "You know, this state I am in...It's all new to me."

Raising my hand slowly, I attempt to touch her. But she backs away.

"Unh uh, pal," she says from the corner of her mouth. "You can't do that."

"Why not?"

"I'm in transition."

"What's that mean exactly?"

"It means I'm not of the earth anymore, but I'm also not of heaven. I'm transitioning."

"Where to?"

"To another life, duh."

"You're going to be born again," I say like a question.

"Here's what I know so far about being...well...not alive," she says. "It's all true. We live again. Until we get it right."

"Does that mean we have the chance to try again? As in you and me?"

Her expression softens.

"You never know." Then, "But before that, you must do something."

"I'm listening."

"Do you still have the key?"

I pull it out of my shirt, holding the leather necklace it's attached to.

"You must find a way to unlock the Golden Kali Statue. Only when you unlock it and open its doors will Kali return to where she belongs in the belly of the statue. For inside the belly of the statue is a portal that leads to a universe unto itself. I know it sounds like something out of 'Close Encounters,' but it really is something you cannot possibly comprehend in your present state."

"My alive flesh-and-blood state here on little old earth."

"Excellent," she says, grinning. "My ex can be taught."

I allow the key to drop back inside my shirt.

"I understand the need to destroy Kali. But what I don't get is why you sent me the key in the first place if you knew you needed it to kill the evil God? Why not hang onto it, and when Kashmiri wasn't looking, insert the key into the statue on your own and destroy the resident evil?"

She shakes her head.

"I knew I wouldn't live long enough to get the chance. Kashmiri's eyes were always on me. So, I made the decision to send it on to the one bad ass person I could trust to get 'er done. Now it's up to you...bad ass."

"How can I possibly get to the statue, Elizabeth?"
She grins again, nods.

"You're Chase Baker," she says. "Famous Renaissance man. You'll find a way. You always do."

Raising her hand, she kisses her fingertips, and blows the kiss my way. I'll be damned if I don't actually feel the kiss on my lips. It's enough to make me cry. She winks at me then turns and begins to walk back into the light. I stand there stunned, paralyzed. In a matter of seconds, she simply vanishes. I feel my eyes grow heavy then, as the concrete corridor begins to close in on me, the light that swallowed up Elizabeth pouring into my nostrils and my open mouth.

Then...

When I come to, I'm lying on my side on the back of a flat-bed truck. Ribs stinging from my dropping onto them, deadweight. Holy crap, I'm definitely not twenty-one anymore. I'm not thirty or forty either. Everything hurts now. As my eyes focus, I can see that Tony is lying beside me, in the back of a pickup truck. But Anjali and the boy are gone.

"Tony," I say, "you awake?"

"Yeah," he says. "I never really passed out from that sleeper gas. I held my breath for as long as I could. The floor opened up, and we took a ride down a metal slide until we finally dropped directly into this truck bed. That fucker, Kashmiri, has thought of everything. You clunked your head and went night-night."

...Just a dream...Elizabeth came to me in a dream...She kissed me in the dream and it felt so real...She gave me instructions. Explicit instructions...

"What about Anjali? The boy?"

"They were removed. I played dead. The bandits took our weapons and the kid and his mother, then left you and me here."

"How long I been out?"

"Two, three minutes. No more."

I feel for my .45. It's gone. But the two sticks of dynamite are still there, shoved deep inside my pants, and hidden by my shirt tail. With my having landed on my stomach and chest, the bandits never saw them. Rather, they never thought to look for them. I sit up, take a better look at the truck. It's a red Toyota 4X4 with a cage set inside the back bed. The cage door, which now takes the place of the truck's tailgate, is padlocked. No wonder they haven't bothered to bind our hands and feet. They'd rather transport us like wild animals.

We're parked in some kind of underground garage that houses other trucks and heavy-duty digging equipment. When the truck's engine fires up and it pulls ahead, I grab hold of the iron bars and pull myself up. The truck proceeds up a ramp to an overhead door that's opening as we're moving towards it so that by the time we reach the top of the concrete ramp it's fully raised.

Pulling out into the hot jungle sun, we follow a gravel road flanked on both sides by Thuggees, their faces masked and the signature yellow sash draped around their waists. All of them screaming in their foreign tongue, their fisted hands raised into the air, their black eyes angry, filled with a hate that seems to emanate from their cells, like a bone deep cancer. Now I see why the Thuggee was the most feared terrorist organization on earth during the nineteenth century. They were the incarnation of evil, as are the men who line this road. They have the power of Satan on their side in the form of Kali, and that makes them a viscous, indestructible, almost superhuman force, at least in their own minds. They also have a God Boy who, through no fault of his own, possess the conduit-like power to conjure up the darkness. There is a fine line between good and evil. Only a razor's edge separates them. One cannot exist without the other, and we possess both in our hearts. If I had to guess, I would say that the God Boy and his mother are about to make the ultimate sacrifice to the evil God, and that Tony and I are right behind them.

Soon, the road comes to an end only a few feet before the open diamond deposit. The truck driver pulls the truck around so that Tony and I face the deposit directly. Chained to the concrete posts is Anjali. Behind her, the statue of Kali has been raised from out of the blue diamond, its eight arms opened wide, six of the hands holding the gold metallic impression of freshly cut out human hearts, one hand holding a curved sword, the final hand holding to the hair of a freshly severed human head. The statue appears to be glowing in the bright shine of the blue diamond like it's about to come alive, just like the stone Kali who attacked us in the depths of the mine.

Parked directly to my right, maybe twenty feet away, is another pickup truck that sports an iron cage on its flatbed. Placed inside it is Rajesh, now dressed in his gold turban, tunic, and trousers. Obviously, Kashmiri is not taking a chance on the God Boy being suddenly rescued by the good guys.

A sea of Thuggees are kneeling before the diamond deposit. They are waving their hands in the air and engaging in charismatic chanting in time with the pounding of drums and the blaring of horns. Now arriving, while surrounded by a special team of red-sashed Thuggees, is Kashmiri. He's back to wearing his ceremonial red robe and the horned head-dress, his face having been painted with red and black stripes. Gripped in his right hand, is the ceremonial wood staff, its head carved in the form of a giant cobra. There's no indication that he's in any pain whatsoever from the round he took in the thigh, or even that he's been shot at all. He moves in a fluid if not graceful manner without so much as a hint of a limp. Maybe Kali has healed his wound. Or, more realistically, perhaps he made the God Boy touch him, and like many others, his bullet wound was mended on the spot.

He takes a moment to bow obediently to the God Boy, then turns back to the diamond deposit, positioning his bare feet on its edge. Anjali's clothing has been removed and now all she wears is a slim white gown. She's struggling against the chains that secure her to the concrete posts, but she is not screaming, as to do so would compromise her integrity, her defiance in the face of certain murder. But with all the chanting and drum beating, it would be impossible to hear her regardless.

"He's gonna cut her heart out," Tony says, grabbing onto the bars beside me. "That son of a bitch is going to cut her, Chase, and there's not a goddamned thing we can do about it."

The sky begins to grow dark, the sun entirely covered up. Lightning strikes off in the distance and the very jungle ground we occupy seems to tremble like a severe aftershock.

"He's summoning the beast," I say. "He doesn't want to use the God Boy's body for his evil purposes. Rather, he's using the boy's good, God-like power as the catalyst for dredging up Kali. In return, he will give Kali Anjali's soul."

"More like he's using the God Boy as bait," Tony points out. "If Kali can swipe the power of a good God and twist it inside out, she'll be even more powerful. Even more evil. I can bet dollars to donuts that with each of these ceremonies, a little bit more of that kid dies."

A cold wind blows. The now blackened sky begins to open up with a pounding rain, and hailstones the size of golf balls.

"We're about to get pummeled, Chase," Tony says, placing his hands on his head.

A bolt of lightning strikes the center of the blue diamond deposit making the diamond glow brilliantly as if a switch has been turned on. Kashmiri raises his head up to the heavens, but I know in my heart that he is speaking to a Satan that resides in the deepest depths of the underworld. The Thuggees are chanting themselves into a frenzy, entirely oblivious of the hailstones pelting them on the head and face, oblivious of the rain, oblivious of the thunder.

Kashmiri lets loose with a scream that turns my blood to ice water. That's when a geyser of steam and a brilliant ray of blue light emanates up from the blue diamond's center, and the giant ghost face of Kali appears, her mouth opened wide and screaming from the depths of her tortured underworld existence. I catch a glance over my shoulder at Rajesh, and I can see that he is down on his back, his six arms and two legs trembling violently while a seizure overtakes his body. Kali is literally sucking the goodness out of the boy along with his life. It's no wonder he's so sickly, so close to death.

Kashmiri's feet levitate off the ground and he begins to float over the diamond deposit toward Anjali and the face of Kali. She spots him and passes out from fright. It's just as well. She need not be conscious for what he's about to do to her.

When he is within inches from her, he pulls the half-moon shaped blade from his sash, presses the tip against Anjali's heart, and at the top of his deep voice, begins to chant something to Kali in a loud voice. It's then that I remember the two sticks of dynamite I have stuffed in my pants.

"TONY, GIVE ME A HAND."

I pull out the first stick and my lighter. I hand him the lighter.

"Fire the bitch up. Then take cover."

The rain and hail pelt our heads.

"Take cover *where* exactly? You'll blow us both to Kingdom Come."

"That woman is about to die. Then we're next. And Kingdom fucking Come is already here 'case you hadn't noticed. Blowing the lock on the cage is our only option."

"Jesus H, does everything have to be so freakin' hard?" he says. "But I will say this, Baker. I forgot how much fun it was hanging out with you."

I hold the stick of dynamite steady, careful to keep it hidden by my bush jacket. In the wind and the rain,

Tony requires both hands to light it up. One to work the lighter and the other cupped hand to shield the flame. The fuse ignites. I take back the lighter and, at the same time, immediately stuff the stick into the U-clasp on the padlock.

"Cover!" I bark.

We jump to the opposite side of the cage, crouch down where the side bars meet the metal floor of the truck bed, shielding our faces with our hands. Even with the fuse spitting out shards of flame, the Thuggees who surround us are so caught up in the trance-inducing ceremony and the appearance of their devil God, they don't take notice of the dynamite. Or, if they notice it, they don't seem to care.

The dynamite blows. The cage shudders and the door bursts open.

"You hit, Tony?" I shout.

"If I am, I don't feel it," he says. "I still got all my limbs?"

"You mean, is your junk still attached?"

He bobs his head, his wide eyes screaming, *I don't believe what just happened*.

"Go," I say. "Go, go."

We jump out and pounce on the two bandits closest to us, relieving them of their Kalashnikovs. We don't give them a chance to warn the others. We shoot them dead on the spot. That gets the attention of a dozen more bandits who turn, aim their weapons. Tony and I hit the dirt and fire into their legs, dropping them where they stand.

In the near distance, Kashmiri is still reciting his chants, preparing to plunge that knife into Anjali's heart. The rain and hail pour down. Lightning strikes all around us, thunder concussions like incoming mortar rounds. The projected face of Kali screams bloody murder directly at me.

Firing from the hip, we make our way to the edge of the diamond deposit.

"Tony, cover me," I order. Then, "Kashmiri!"

The red-robed and black-bearded man turns, his knife still in hand.

I don't waste any time with the terrorist. I plant a bead and shoot. But the rifle is out of rounds. The Chief Thuggee's face lights up with pleasure as he returns the dagger to his sash, and hurls himself across the diamond deposit, wrapping both his hands around my throat.

Behind me, it's all Tony can do to keep the bandits back. Shooting until his rifle is empty, then picking up another one and shooting it until that, too, is empty.

I fall onto my back, Kashmiri landing hard on my chest. I punch him in the mouth with all the force I can muster. But it's like punching a brick wall. He raises his entire body up effortlessly so that he's straddling me on his knees. He pulls the crescent dagger back out of his sash, presses the blade against my neck with one hand, and grabs hold of the Kali Key with the other, yanking on the thick leather necklace in effort to break it as if it were a worn shoelace.

"Kali claims your soul!" he chants, his smile beaming. "Kali claims your soul!"

Knowing that strength alone won't break the leather necklace, Kashmiri pulls the blade away from my neck and starts to cut.

"Chase, I can't hold them," Tony barks from behind me. "There's too many."

I hear a scream. Peering over my shoulder, I see that Tony has taken a bullet to the chest. He drops hard, like a sack of rocks. That's when I feel for the last stick of dynamite stuffed in my waistband. I pull it out, along with my lighter and, cupping my hand around it so that Kashmiri can't see it, fire up the fuse. I wait the few seconds it takes for the fuse to burn down to the explosive. Raising the business end of the lighter up to Kashmiri's neck, I flick the flame under his chin. His mouth opens wide while he screams in agony. He releases the necklace and the dagger.

"Eat this!" I say, stuffing the stick of dynamite into his mouth and down his throat.

I roll my body out from under him.

The stick detonates.

When I turn to look, I see that Kashmiri's head has evaporated along with most of his chest cavity. His big body absorbed almost the entire blast. The exploded dynamite has had another more profound effect. It's caused the army of Thuggees to back-step away from the diamond deposit, some of the black-clad men even throwing down their weapons and running away towards the forest that surrounds the grassy plain. Now that their invincible leader has been so easily destroyed, they know that they too are next in line for a one-way ticket to the underworld.

But the devil has already been summoned, even without the sacrificial offering of Anjali's beating heart. Before me, floating above the still unconscious body of the God Boy's mother is the face of Kali. The gaunt, hollow-eyed skull screams in anger. The earth shakes once more. Lightning strikes all around me.

..."*You must find a way to unlock the Golden Kali Statue. Only when you unlock it and open its doors will Kali return to where she belongs. In the belly of the statue.*"

I feel for the key around my neck. I cross over the trembling diamond, the heat that's radiating up from it shooting up through the soles of my boots all the way up my legs and into my spine. I pass by the concrete pillars supporting the chains that bind Anjali until I come to the ancient Kali statue. Pulling the diamond embedded bronze key from my neck, I eyeball the back of the solid gold statue. There's a rectangle embossed into the statue's back. Some sort of writing or inscription is inlaid inside the box, along with a small, narrow slit that's intended to facilitate a key. I slip the key inside.

The gold statue shakes and comes alive, its legs straightening out, its eight arms moving up and down, its eyes blinking, mouth opening and closing. The hearts gripped in six of its hands are now real, alive, pumping and bleeding. The blade of the sword gripped in the seventh hand is waving, the rain and hail spattering against it. The severed head being held by its hair in the eighth hand is suddenly alive, its eyes blinking, its mouth moving, as if trying to say something.

The skull on the Kali statue splits open, like a rose coming into full bloom. That's when the giant, radiating ghost of Kali begins to distort and change shape, like the bulbs on a stadium light show suddenly losing their power. The translucent ghost image grows thinner and thinner, then smaller and smaller, like a black hole collapsing into itself until finally it is sucked into the statue head, the skull panels slamming closed with a resounding bang that echoes throughout the valley.

The radiation from the blue diamond quickly disappears along with its heat while the rain and hail stop, the black cloud-covered sky opening up to reveal a heavenly blue. My eyes locked on the Golden Kali Statue, I see its once glowing skin now burst into flames while the entire eight-armed body disintegrates into a pile of charred ash. The wind blows the ash around so that it covers the blue diamond deposit like fallen leaves on a glass blue pond.

Anjali raises her head then, says, "Am I alive?"

"Yes, you are alive," I say. Peering over my left shoulder. "Tony," I whisper, staring at the pool of blood that surrounds his body.

The Thuggees are running away from the diamond mine. Running for their evil lives. I cross over the diamond, grab hold of Tony's Kalishnikov, carry it with me back across the diamond deposit to Anjali.

"Let's just get you away from here first," I say. "Then we'll find a key that will remove the shackles."

I press the barrel of the Kalashnikov against the chain that holds Anjali's left arm to the first concrete pillar. I shoot and the chain breaks free. I do the same with the second arm and the second pillar. When Anjali is released, she runs to the cage where her boy is lying on his back, unconscious.

"Rajesh!" she wails, "Rajesh. Are you alive?"

I cross over the blue diamond, but stop when I come to Kashmiri. Digging under his sash, I find his key ring. I carry them to Anjali and unlock her wrist shackles. She hardly notices when they drop to the ground. It takes me several tries, but within a few seconds I find the key that opens Rajesh's cage. As soon as the steel barred door is open, Anjali reaches in and pulls him out, cradling him to her.

His big, brown eyes open then, and he works up a smile. But that smile quickly vanishes when he spots Tony lying on his back on the ground.

"Please put me down," the six-armed God Boy says as Anjali lowers him to the ground. He slowly makes the few steps to where Tony is laid out.

VINCENT ZANDRI

Dropping to his knees, the boy lays all of his hands on my now dead friend. For a moment, I interpret Rajesh's gesture as one of respect and thanks for a man who helped save his life and in return, gave his own life. But nothing short of miraculous happens then. A dull glow emanates from all of Rajesh's hands, his body transforming from sickly boy to a holy spirit-filled entity. A being filled with the goodness and the glory of a benevolent god. In turn, Tony's body trembles, the blood that surrounds him disappears, and slowly, he sits up. The man, not reincarnated, but resurrected.

"Holy cow," he says. "Anybody get the license plate on the truck that just plowed me over?"

Holy cow...pun entirely intended, right Tony?

My eyes fill with tears. Dr. Singh did not lie about the power in Rajesh. His power of good over evil. His gift for raising up the dead with just a single touch. If only he'd been able to touch Elizabeth, she might be here with us now. But the kid was locked in a cage. How awful it must have been for the God Boy to know he could have saved her life...so many lives that were sacrificed here...and not be able to do a damn thing about it.

Rajesh is Brahma...Brahma is Rajesh...

Rajesh turns and goes to his mother. Once again, she receives him in her arms like she is never going to let him go.

"Mother," he says. "I had such a terrible dream. I dreamt that the evil Kali returned to earth along with an army of evil men dressed all in black...the terrible Thuggee."

"It was all a dream, Rajesh," Anjali says, pulling away his turban and running her hand through his thick black hair. "It's all right now. It was only a dream."

Tony approaches me, his eyes wide. There's blood on his shirt, but no longer is there an entry or exit wound. Together, we take a step or two backward, to get a better look at the diamond deposit.

"You sure what happened here was just a dream?" Tony says. "Because I swear I took a bullet not five minutes ago. Although, I could be wrong about that. Maybe somebody just hit me in the chest with a rock." He pauses for a moment as if needing time for the reality of what just happened to him to sink in. Then, "But if somebody told me they'd witnessed a giant evil see-through skull projecting itself from out of the earth by means of a gigantic blue diamond, a golden statue, and an evil high priest who levitates, I'd say, take another sip why don't ya."

"I didn't see anything like that happening," I say. "Did you?"

"Save that stuff for your novels."

"I'm already writing it in my head."

Then, coming from above, an armada of Blackhawk choppers. Slowing to a hover, they open up with their nose-mounted Gatling guns on the escaping Thuggees. In the end, it's a turkey shoot while the evil terrorist cult is stopped dead in its tracks out in the open field.

"Hell's gonna be busy today," Tony says.

"Hell for bad people," I say. "Heaven for good."

EPILOGUE

ANOTHER CHOPPER APPEARS ON THE SCENE. THIS ONE A Huey that, like the Blackhawks, bears the signature red Star of David and trident crest of the Nepalese army. It sets down only a few feet away from the big blue diamond. Emerging from it is Dr. Singh, neatly attired in a white Nehru jacket and matching pants. First he goes to Anjali and Rajesh, hugging both of them tightly, clearly relieved to see that not only have they survived, but they appear to be in relative good health. He then releases the two and approaches Tony and me, a broad smile planted on his face.

"Why is it the good guys always show up after the battle?" Tony whispers.

"Shush," I say. "This good guy has a thick wallet, and he owes us big time. You've got an office and a bar to rebuild, remember?"

"You've done a splendid job, Mr. Baker," Singh

says, holding out his hand. "However will I reward you?"

"You'll get a bill," I say. "Don't you worry." I take his hand in mine, shake it.

"Don't forget that little bit about Rudy being dead and my bar burning down," Tony says. The old excavator tosses me a wink and a sly smile. He then places some fresh chew in his cheek, excuses himself, heads back toward Anjali and the God Boy.

Singh turns to me.

"I am truly sorry for your loss," he says, pursing his lips. "But I see Anjali and the boy are safe."

"It must have been a tough thing to swallow," I say, "knowing Anjali was with Kashmiri and that the relationship, however brief, would lead directly to the boy's abduction."

He nods, the look on his face like I'm opening a deep wound that never healed in the first place. "She truly had no idea regarding the depth of his evil intentions. But then, she doesn't need any chastising from the likes of me...the man who left them in the first place. She already blames herself for what happened. I suspect she will go to her grave bearing the burden of that guilt. That's why she insisted on accompanying you on the mission. She knew it was dangerous. But if she died while trying to save her son's life, then that final act would at least absolve her soul of permanent damnation."

"And what about you?" I say. "How deep does your guilt go for having left Anjali and Rajesh when they needed you most?"

The skin on his normally coffee-with-milk colored face turns pale.

"You have to ask that question, Mr. Baker?"

"That kind of child handicap can place great

strain on a family," I say. "Rajesh was cast out, considered a freak. It must have been difficult for a man of your power and prestige. So then, it must have come as quite a shock when suddenly the entire Hindu world went from treating Rajesh as a freak to a God."

He nods contemplatively.

"We all seek perfection, Mr. Baker," he says. "In both ourselves and in our children. But I am ashamed I left when I did. And it is something I will have to live with for the rest of my days. So you see, my chance at achieving perfection is forever vanished."

...You're being too tough on the guy, Chase. You're no better than he is...

"I know the feeling, pal. I have a daughter in New York. I too have to live with the fact that I don't see her enough." In my head, I see the spunky little long-haired girl in her short dress and sneakers, running off to school or the park. "We all make decisions and then we have to live with them."

He bites down on his bottom lip. "We get another chance if we don't get it right in this life. If you believe in that kind of thing."

"Right you are, Doc. If it doesn't happen in this life, Dharma or Brahma or whoever will see to it that you get another chance, and another, and another, until you get it right...Like you said, if you believe in the sort of thing."

"Something like that."

"And now, you not only get your son back," I say, "but you claim quite the prize for Nepal. The lost Diamond Mine of India...which, it just so happens, is located in Nepal."

"Or perhaps the Lost Diamond Mine of India is indeed waiting to be discovered in India along with another Golden Kali Statue. Perhaps it makes this find look like the corner jewelry shop." His face assumes a smile. Because his story has a happy ending. But I can't say the same for mine.

"Elizabeth died for the statue that marked the location of this blue diamond mine," I say. "She spent her whole life in pursuit of the Golden Kali Statue. If she hadn't sent me the bronze key, Anjali would be dead now. Maybe Rajesh, too."

"I understand you are grieving, Mr. Baker. Grieving for a second time."

"Once was enough, Singh," I say. "Elizabeth gave up on me, even if I never stopped loving her. She's in a better place than you and me."

He purses his lips.

"On this day, a baby will be born somewhere in the world, and it will bear the soul of Elizabeth. She will graduate from the transition phase to the earthly life phase once more. If you believe that...believe it with all your heart and soul like I do...then she is far from dead. She lives, all over again."

A wave of warmth pours over my body. Makes me shiver for a second or two.

"Here's what I know so far about being...well...not alive," she says. "It's all true. We live again. Until we get it right."

I hold out my hand. Singh takes it in his. Shakes. Releasing it, he heads across the blue diamond deposit to his ex-wife and child.

The God Boy.

I stare up at the blue sky and I see the face of Elizabeth staring back at me. See her smile, her green eyes, her lovely hair. Singh was right all along. She never really died in the first place. Elizabeth is about to live again.

"I'll see you soon, babe," I whisper. "In this life or the next."

To one day have a second chance with Elizabeth...

...That's all the reward a jerk like me will ever need.

THE END

If you enjoyed this Chase Baker Thriller, please explore *The Shroud Key* (Chase Baker No.1) and *Chase Baker and the Golden Condor* (Chase Baker No. 2)

ABOUT THE AUTHOR

VINCENT ZANDRI is the *New York Times* and *USA Today* bestselling author of more than sixteen novels, including *Everything Burns*, *The Innocent*, *The Remains*, *Orchard Grove*, and *The Shroud Key*. He is also the author of the ITW Thriller Award winning and Shamus Award nominated Dick Moonlight PI series. A freelance photojournalist and solo traveler, he is the founder of the blog *The Vincent Zandri Vox*. He lives in New York and Florence, Italy. For more, go to http://www.vincentzandri.com/.

.

CPSIA information can be obtained
at www.ICGtesting.com
Printed in the USA
BVHW031050181019
561475BV00003B/598/P